"Do you really want to chance working with me?" Willa asked.

Nick didn't miss the vulnerability in her voice. "I want your help, if you're willing to give it."

"Yes, but it's just that we obviously don't agree on everything." Nick raised an eyebrow, a dry smile on his lips. Willa felt she'd received a precious gift at the return of warmth to his eyes. Allowing herself a small smile, she added, "Well, you have to admit, every time we're together for more than ten minutes, we either end up arguing or—kissing." Desire flashed in Nick's eyes and consumed her with heat.

With a sexy grin, he said, "I'm willing to run the risk if you are." Then he sealed the bargain with his mouth pressed to hers in a sizzling embrace. . . .

WHAT ARE *LOVESWEPT* ROMANCES?

They are stories of true romance and touching emotion. We believe those two very important ingredients are constants in our highly sensual and very believable stories in the LOVESWEPT line. Our goal is to give you, the reader, stories of consistently high quality that may sometimes make you laugh, sometimes make you cry, but are always fresh and creative and contain many delightful surprises within their pages.

Most romance fans read an enormous number of books. Those they truly love, they keep. Others may be traded with friends and soon forgotten. We hope that each LOVESWEPT romance will be a treasure—a "keeper." We will always try to publish

LOVE STORIES YOU'LL NEVER FORGET
BY AUTHORS YOU'LL ALWAYS REMEMBER

The Editors

Loveswept® 651

ILLEGAL MOTION

DONNA KAUFFMAN

BANTAM BOOKS

NEW YORK • TORONTO • LONDON • SYDNEY • AUCKLAND

ILLEGAL MOTION
A Bantam Book / November 1993

If you would be interested in receiving protective vinyl covers for your Loveswept books, please write to this address for information:

Loveswept
Bantam Books
P.O. Box 985
Hicksville, NY 11802

ISBN 0-553-44379-8

Published simultaneously in the United States and Canada

PRINTED IN THE UNITED STATES OF AMERICA

OPM   0 9 8 7 6 5 4 3 2 1

Special thanks to Joyce and Ellen for
reading . . . and reading. . . .
And to my family and friends for their
unfailing support.

This book is dedicated to my husband,
Jeff—you were right, I can do this.

PROLOGUE

"As the charges against you stem from evidence obtained without a properly issued search warrant, I have no choice but to dismiss this case. Mr. Logan, you are free to go."

The pounding of Judge Hanover's gavel was lost in the cacophony of angry shouts and groans of disappointment from spectators packing the courtroom.

Nick Logan rose slowly from his chair at the defense table, wincing as he straightened the injured knee that had stiffened painfully during the long morning session. Frowning, he retrieved his briefcase. He should be overjoyed that he'd be leaving the courtroom without cold bracelets around his wrists, but he wasn't. Justice hadn't been done. And he wouldn't be truly free until he could prove he was innocent.

Murmuring a thank-you to his attorney, he picked up his cane, then started up the aisle. A legion of reporters was sure to be waiting on the other side of the heavy swinging doors and he mentally prepared himself to face them. Those reporters certainly wouldn't be fawning over him the way they had just the previous year when he'd helped the Jaguars win their second consecutive Super Bowl. No. They'd keep on attacking him as they had since the police had conveniently discovered packets of cocaine in his locker the day after he'd failed the NFL's supposedly foolproof drug test.

The moment he emerged into the corridor, flashing lights blinded him while a thunder of questions assaulted his ears. Head held high, Nick threaded his way through the crowd. He tamped down his temper and the urge to tell the media his side of the story. It wouldn't help. He'd come off looking as though he was out to get sympathy . . . or worse, that he was an outright liar. Pride was the only thing he had left.

Pride and Skylar Buchanan. Not for the first time Nick sent up a silent prayer of thanks for his college buddy. While the rest of the world believed Nick was just another overpaid jock who'd let success as an all-pro offensive tackle go to his head—and up his nose—Sky had gone out of his way to be supportive and to ferret out the truth.

Dazzling spring sunshine bounced off windshields and chrome as Nick picked his way through the cars in the lot and found his sedan. He tossed his briefcase and cane onto the passenger's seat and carefully angled his six-foot-four-inch frame under the steering wheel. He smiled. Now that he wouldn't be appealing a conviction from a jail cell, he could take a more active role in clearing his name. And he had a lot to work with. He and Sky had followed leads to one name, one startling name: Eric Miller. The Jaguars' star quarterback just might be the man who had framed Nick. Sky had taken a job with the only person who might be able to give them conclusive proof—Eric's lover at the time of Nick's arrest: Willa Trask.

Out on the open road, Nick floored the accelerator, all pretense at patience gone.

ONE

Nick was frowning as he followed the winding corridor of the Millennium Sports Club to the weight room, where Sky had said to meet him. A fruitless and frustrating week had passed since his case had been dismissed. He'd come straight to the club from the airport; his trip to New York to appeal personally to the commissioner of football for reinstatement had been a failure.

His frown deepening into a scowl, Nick recalled the gratingly polite way the commissioner had dismissed him and his request for the ban to be rescinded so he'd be eligible to play for the Jaguars in the fall. Damn. The man wouldn't even listen to him or his explanations. Nick vowed not to waste another minute. He had to clear his name. And fast. Thank God for Sky. He'd left a message on Nick's machine that he had important new information and asking for a meeting at the club.

Hearing Sky's unmistakable voice, Nick hesitated before opening the weight-room door.

"I don't . . . think I can . . . get it up . . . again."

"Sure you can. Come on, concentrate" came a feminine voice that was soft yet deep and brooked no argument. "You can do it, Sky. Now push. Push."

The urge to find out who belonged to that intriguing voice of pure honey mixed with pure steel was irresistible. But Nick wasn't one to invade a man's privacy at a potentially delicate moment. He waited a discreet few seconds, then said loudly before cracking the door, "So Sky Buchanan can't get it up again?" He eased into the cavernous room and stopped dead in his tracks.

A gorgeous, sexy redhead stood behind the weight bench where Sky was working out. Startled by Nick's voice, she had straightened up and was looking directly at him.

The woman was tall, exceptionally fit, and slim. Her breasts were full, soft curves that pressed against the mint-green sweatsuit she wore. The sleeves had been cut out of the shirt, revealing two well-toned arms; the loose-fitting pants obscured the shape of her extremely long legs. His attention returned to her crowning glory, lingering on the strands of bright auburn hair escaping the band holding it away from her face. The curling wisps of hair clinging to her damp skin along with the memory of her caramel-coated voice made Nick forget his urgent need to talk with Sky. The woman took his breath away. His sudden desire for the striking redhead surprised him. Since his college days playing ball, he'd attracted the opposite sex like nectar drew bees. But it hadn't taken long after turning pro for him to learn that the major reason a lot of women wanted to get into his bed was because he was a famous ballplayer. Bragging rights about sexual conquests weren't the exclusive territory of men, he'd discovered. As a result, he'd become very selective.

Annoyed at being so easily sidetracked, Nick decided to get to the matter that had brought him to the club. To do so, he had to brush off the redhead.

"Millennium is certainly a ritzy enough health club, Sky, but the weight room?" The deliberately sarcastic edge to his voice worked as he'd hoped; the woman seemed more than a little annoyed. "You should have chosen something more seductive," he went on. "The steam room, maybe? Of course, atmosphere isn't everything, but most women require at least a pretense of class."

No longer irritated, the redhead's expression turned to one of full-fledged anger. Nick belatedly realized that Sky's taste in women must have changed. Judging from her stiffened spine and lifted chin, he could tell she was no fawning groupie—which meant there would be no practiced pout or flouncing out in a calculated chase-me-down-and-apologize huff.

His regret over his less than polite tactics must have shown on his face, because Ms. Sexy Voice's expression changed from anger to resigned tolerance. She started to speak, but was interrupted by a loud groan.

The barbell hovered dangerously over Sky's head for a moment before she snapped to attention and guided the heavily weighted iron bar to the rack in front of her. "Sky, I'm sorry," she said, her voice even huskier than before. She fired an accusing glare at Nick before turning back to Sky, who was now sitting up and mopping at the sweat on his forehead. "I wasn't . . . I mean . . . he distracted . . . Sorry," she finished lamely.

When she looked back at Nick, her anger had returned full force. He was too far away to see the color of her eyes, but with her russet-red hair he'd lay odds on green.

Blazing green.

"Mister, I don't know who you are, or how you got in here after hours," she stated clearly, her deep voice all steel now, "but in the future please be more careful about startling people around heavy weights. It's dangerous and could result in serious injury." Her pointed look left no doubt as to who the injured party would be.

Truly regretting his earlier words, Nick realized his error in judgment even more. She'd handled his rudeness—crudeness, really—very professionally, earning respect and an apology. Caught up in dealing with his continued fascination with her, Nick was a beat late recognizing how odd the expression on Sky's face was.

"It's okay, Willa," Sky said. "I told Kelly to let him in before she left for the night. He *usually* has better manners." He shot Nick a quelling look, silently urging him to keep his cool. "But I still claim him as a friend." His smile tight at the corners, Sky gestured Nick over to them. "Willa Trask, meet Nick Logan, former college football teammate and a major cramp in my style."

Willa Trask! This was Willa Trask? Nick's mind raced as the news sank in. He fought a hard-won battle to maintain a calm facade, extremely difficult considering he was looking at the woman who had very possibly helped Eric Miller ruin his career.

He glanced from Willa to Sky, whose massive shoulders lifted in an apologetic shrug. Not trusting himself to speak, Nick grabbed his cane and crossed the room, buying some much-needed time to collect himself.

Willa Trask. He'd been looking directly at her when Sky introduced him. Not a flicker of recognition had crossed her lovely face. She was good, he thought, real good. Nick studied her carefully, his stony expression giving no indication of his inner turmoil.

"You must be a really good friend," she said, her whiskey voice holding his full attention, "if Sky is willing to overlook the fact that because of you, I almost let three hundred pounds of iron come crashing down on his chest." She looked back at Sky. "I really *am* sorry. I'm not usually so easily distracted."

A year ago Nick would have been delighted to be a "distraction" to a beautiful redhead, but not now—and most certainly not under these circumstances with Willa Trask. He stopped a few feet away from the weight bench, cursing himself for his stupidity. He and Sky had talked about charming the lovely Ms. Trask into incriminating herself. And while she was a damn sight more intriguing than he'd expected, Nick doubted if this queen bee would go for his nectar after his rude performance.

Nick racked his brain, trying to find some way to rectify the situation and turn it to his advantage. But it was hard to concentrate. He was still dealing with the fact that she hadn't shown the least bit of guilt, not even a shred of discomfort, when Sky introduced him. She looked as though she'd never even heard of Nick Logan, much less helped to destroy his life.

Well, if he'd faced off against some of the toughest men in the NFL and never backed down, he could sure as hell jar her out of her cold, calculating control.

His knee started to cramp from tension, and Nick forced himself to relax. He tried to smile, hoping he looked disarmingly sexy. Judging from Sky's expression, he wasn't succeeding. Either way it made no difference. Willa had already turned away to collect her towel and Millennium gym bag.

Nick's frown returned as he watched her walk to the locker-room door. It was on the tip of his tongue to stop her graceful exit with a few pointed questions, but before he had a chance, she turned back. Her expression was unreadable, but her voice when she spoke was tight, her tone clipped.

"After years spent working in a male-dominated field, I don't usually defend myself against macho innuendo." She paused for a moment, as if choosing her words very carefully. "But I will say this—I'm a manager of this club, and if you had spoken to one of our guests like you spoke to me earlier, friend or not, you'd have been out of here within ten seconds."

Nick tightened his grip on his cane and on his emotions. He caught Sky's look of warning out of the corner of his eye and gritted his teeth against the urge to tell her exactly what he thought of her. *That* would definitely have earned him a quick exit!

Sky quickly jumped in to dispel the tension. "Why don't we call it a night, Willa? Nick probably wants to talk football, and after an evening with me, I'm sure that's one subject you're sick to death of." He stood, quietly cuing her to leave.

Willa nodded, carefully avoiding Nick's gaze. "I'll see you tomorrow, Sky." She started to push through the large oak door, but at the last second she paused and looked back over her shoulder, pinning Nick with her gaze. "See how much quicker you get results when you ask nicely?" She was gone before he could respond.

An already bad day had just gotten much worse. Nick rounded on his friend. "Why the hell didn't you tell me she'd be here? I just made a complete ass of myself!"

"Sorry I couldn't warn you. I really thought Willa and I would be done long before you got here. Things didn't go too well with the old commish, huh?" When Nick just glared, Sky added, "I didn't do it on purpose, Nick."

Nick's anger dissipated. "I know." He heaved a sigh, raking his fingers through his already unruly black hair. "I guess with the commissioner's dripping concern for my continuing drug rehabilitation, then this . . . Though I should've guessed she wasn't one of your women." Nick chuckled. "I knew right off she was too classy for the disreputable likes of you."

"Look who's talking," Sky shot back. Pulling his towel from his shoulders, he snapped it at Nick's chest. "When was the last time you got your hair cut anyway?"

Nick ran a hand through the mass of dark curls that fell over the collar of his tailored black suit. "The length of my hair has been the least of my worries lately. Of course, if it offends your delicate sensibilities and obvious fashion sense . . ." Nick aimed a look at the huge tear in the knee of Sky's aged sweats. His hulking friend was an ad for Goodwill.

"I know it's not in line with Millennium

standards, but since my boss didn't care, I . . ." Sky's comment trailed off as Nick's smile disappeared. "She's not what you expected, is she?" Not waiting for an answer, he added, "I know how you feel. When we learned she was the one seen delivering small packages to Miller at the Jags' practice field, I fully expected we'd confront a calculating ice princess."

Nick shot his friend an incredulous look. "You're saying she's not? She seems like one cool customer to me. She didn't even blink when you said my name." He shifted his weight slightly, leaning more heavily on his cane, then gave in and sat on the bench opposite Sky. The tension had made the throbbing in his knee unbearable.

"Yeah, she's confused me too. I've gotten the impression since I've been here that she's just an honest, hardworking lady. I know she doesn't date. The word is she's still hurting over her breakup with Miller."

Nick snorted. "Bet it burned her good when Miller dumped her after he'd gotten what he wanted. She helps him pass the drug test by framing me so he can keep his almighty income, then her meal ticket walks out."

"I don't know, Nick. Now that I know her, I just can't picture her setting up an innocent man." Sky avoided Nick's angry gaze by ducking his head for a moment. After a deep breath he added, "I know that her connection to Eric and the team doctor *does* seem a bit too coincidental. I just wonder if someone besides Doc Abbott could be the link to switching the test results."

"Sky, between being buddies with Doc Abbott and delivering those nice little packages to Eric at training camp, Willa Trask had to have been into the frame all the way up to her sexy green eyeballs." Massaging his knee, Nick added quickly, "But that's old news. What've you found out?"

"Things could get interesting here real quick. Willa has been instrumental in setting up a new program for the local pros to train at Millennium during off-seasons. Guess who signed up today?"

Nick didn't have to guess. "Eric Miller."

"Got it in one. I overheard the receptionist swooning over the fact that Mr. Golden Arm is coming in Monday."

"Well, then I have to get busy, don't I? Before the gruesome twosome screw some other poor, unsuspecting sap out of a career. Seeing me didn't have her falling all over herself with guilt, and my big mouth has probably sabotaged my plan of wining and dining the truth out of Ms. Trask. She doesn't look like the type who'd cave in under intimidation. No doubt she'd just lie to save her own skin."

Sky groaned at the wicked smile on Nick's face. "The last time I saw that look, Lawrence Taylor ended up spending the second half on the sidelines."

"Well, Ms. Trask will probably be at least as formidable as L.T., maybe even harder to bench." His smile hardened a bit as he glanced down at two of the more tangible rewards of a successful career, proudly displayed on his scarred fingers. "But I've got a lot more riding on this than a shot at another Super Bowl ring." The gleam in his eyes reflected his fierce pride and determination as he faced Sky. "If Ms. Trask wants to mend broken athletes, then she can start by working on this knee of mine."

Oh my God, what did I do? Willa gripped the frame of the heavy oak door for support. At that moment the old saying about eavesdroppers never hearing anything good about themselves seemed an understatement.

Her mind reeled at the implications of what she'd overheard. A swirl of sickening dread coiled in her stomach as she slowly admitted to herself that Nick Logan's suspicions could very easily be true.

Eric Miller. That conniving jerk. She recalled his endless questions about her friendship with Doc, and all of those packages she'd delivered that he'd claimed were just vitamin supplements. It all came together with horrific clarity.

"But I didn't know," she whispered against the palm of her hand. Until a few minutes ago Nick Logan had meant no more to her than a name on the Jags' roster. She vaguely recalled the media hubbub over a local star being arrested for possession of drugs, but she hadn't paid attention. After her painful breakup with Eric, she'd made a point of avoiding local sports news, especially anything concerning the Jaguars.

Her emotions rioting, she tried to calm herself and concentrate on the past. Because of her heavy class schedule, she'd visited Doc less than usual last year, but she couldn't recall meeting any players. Except Eric. How had Nick even found out about her? She was certain from his brief look of shock that he'd never seen *her* before, either. Her dates with Eric had never included any of his teammates.

Reacting on instinct, she started to go back into the training room, ready to tell Nick her side of the story and offer her help. But the impulse died quickly as she remembered his mocking smile and the hard certainty she'd heard in his deep voice as he'd talked about her with Sky.

Willa needed to sort things out before she faced Nick. She was almost running by the time she reached the sanctuary of her office.

Once inside, she quickly closed the door, then leaned heavily against it. Instead of focusing on Eric and her implied guilt, her mind conjured up the image of Nick Logan. Even lounging in the doorway, he'd exuded power. From the thick mass of dark curls that trailed over his snowy-white collar to the broad shoulders encased in a black suit jacket that couldn't have come off a rack, leaning on a cane that looked so incongruous next to thighs noticeably well developed, even in tailored pants. He made her feel petite. She had to admit it had been a strangely pleasant sensation. Around most men, her five-foot-ten-inch frame made her feel gawky and unfeminine. Yet after spending most of her twenty-five years around gyms and training centers, she'd seen plenty of well-built bodies.

No, it wasn't his size that intimidated her. She was an expert on dealing with people who thought of intimidation as a career asset. It was his sheer presence. Eyes the brilliant blue of a cold mountain lake; the glittering surface enticing, but with something darker, more menacing lying just beneath. His scrutiny had been so unnerving that if she hadn't been angry at leaving Sky unspotted, she doubted she'd have been able to string two coherent words together.

Willa tilted her head back against the door, then jumped at the sound of someone knocking on it. She barely had time to turn around before it inched open. The piercing blue eyes of Nick Logan met hers. And his flashing grin threw her off balance. Pulling her gaze away from him, she turned and walked behind her desk. Assuming he was here for a confrontation, she purposely sat down.

But as she watched him walk toward her and sit in the chair directly across the desk, she prayed he wouldn't call her bluff.

When he finally spoke, the contrite tone of his voice was at direct odds with the flash of light in his eyes. "Sorry to barge in, but could you spare a minute? I'd like to have a word with you."

Willa managed a brief nod, knowing if she tried to speak she'd reveal how nervous he made her. His distracting presence in the training room dimmed next to dealing with him in the suddenly close confines of her office. Too late she realized her expression had given her away.

Nick watched as she pieced her control together. For an instant the cool composure she'd maintained in the training room with such ease vanished. Underneath he found traces of fear and vulnerability. If he wasn't mistaken, he also saw a flash of awareness that had him reconsidering his original plan to charm and disarm. Had she just remembered who he was? Renewed anger shot through him. Was ruining a man's career so insignificant that she could have forgotten?

Willa watched the quick play of emotions cross his face. Close up, the charming smile seemed strained and she could almost feel his frustration. Deciding she'd waited long enough, she said, "It's late and I'd really like to get home. If you've come to apologize, please don't. Believe me, I've dealt with your type before." That was a lie; she'd never dealt with anyone like Nick Logan.

"Please, call me Nick. And what exactly is my type?"

Willa refused to answer or let herself be drawn in by the sexy flash of white teeth. Obviously Mr. Logan could change moods like a chameleon changed colors when it suited his purpose. And she was painfully aware of his purpose. "Listen, I know you're a friend of Sky's, and that you probably joke with him like that all the time, but I don't happen to find such remarks very funny.

Please don't insult me further with insincere apologies."

"Who said I came here to apologize?" he drawled, letting his gaze break away from her widening green eyes to travel slowly downward, lingering on her slightly parted lips. "Actually, I wanted to talk business," he went on, his tone more serious, but the knowing grin still playing at the corners of his mouth. "Sky tells me you're one of the best sports therapists around, and as you can see"—Nick used his cane to point to his knee—"I definitely need you."

Willa stiffened at his softly spoken request. There was no denying he'd intended his blunt proposal to sound seductive. Or did she just want it to be? She risked a glance at his face. The sexy smile hadn't warmed his blue eyes, or softened the tiny strain lines etched at the corners.

No, she had no desire to get tangled up with Nick Logan. Being used once was one time too many. She'd help him clear his name, if only to clear hers as well, but she would do it on her own terms.

Breaking eye contact, she flipped open her schedule book. "I'm afraid I won't be available, as I'm starting a new program here on Monday. But we have many other competent therapists and trainers. Richard could—"

"I don't want Richard. I want you."

Willa's heart jumped in her throat. He'd risen and was leaning over the desk.

The combination of his nearness and the husky way he'd said *I want you* proved he intended to fight dirty. Before she could think of how to put the distance back between them, he reached over and placed a blunt fingertip on the schedule. He traced over the column with her name at the top until he found a white space. Shifting his weight onto her desk, he craned his neck to read the tiny print in the margin.

"Monday morning, eleven o'clock. Sounds good to me."

Refusing to look up, she tightened her grasp on the pencil, hoping it would snap before her temper did. "Mr. Logan," she began, her voice tight. The rest of the sentence died when he pried the pencil from her fingers and filled in his name, a series of dark slashes against the white page.

"Just Nick," he said, repeating the name he'd written. "I'm sure you'll remember who I am."

Nick laid the pencil down and eased his weight off of the desk, uncomfortably aware, and not a little annoyed, that the light fragrance she wore had tempted him to lean even closer. Maybe she was better at this game than he'd given her credit for. He quickly reined in his wayward thoughts, amazed that she'd managed to get to him like this. It made him wonder how she'd let Miller slip away. He turned away from unsettling thoughts of her in Eric's arms. So she was gorgeous and smelled good. Just made his goal that much less distasteful to achieve.

Yet somehow her warm-as-wine voice and that vulnerable look he'd witnessed as he'd barged into her office kept twining together in his mind. He couldn't help thinking that if anything was distasteful, it was what he planned to do to her.

"I'm really sorry, but I have to schedule you with someone else."

"Why, Willa? I'm only asking you to help me set up a program. I've rehabilitated from knee surgery before, so it'll only take one or two sessions for a start. Surely you can fit me in." Her confident gaze faltered a little and he pressed his small advantage. "Sky wouldn't have recommended you if he thought someone else could do better."

Willa wanted to tell him she knew exactly why he wouldn't settle for anyone but her. She'd never been good at lies or half-truths, and the way Nick threw her off balance with a mere glance and a smile told her she'd never be able to keep up the pretense if she was forced to work so closely with him.

The phone rang and she grabbed it, glad for the temporary reprieve. "Millennium Sports Club. Ms. Trask."

Nick used the interruption to ease himself back into the chair. The sudden edge in her tone caught his attention and he looked up just in time to see her entire body go rigid. He felt his muscles tighten as the lovely flush drained from her face, leaving her skin almost white.

"What do you want?" Willa struggled to sound calm. Eric Miller had a voice that could charm the skin off a snake—or the clothes off a woman. She took some pride in the fact that his velvety tone now made her stomach knot. "What do you want?" she repeated.

She could picture Eric's perfect wounded pout as he answered. "I thought since I'd be seeing you again when I come in on Monday, it would be nice if we could act like adults. I'd like to take you to dinner, give us a chance to talk things over before I show up at the club. I've really changed, Willa, and I guess I wanted to spare you any embarrassment. You know how people love to gossip."

It was just like Eric to assume that she'd been unable to keep her private life a secret. Act like adults? It was also just like him to try to make her feel like an immature child by not agreeing to see him again. After all, her immaturity and lack of womanly wiles had been his excuse for cheating on her when she'd found him with another woman. And she'd believed him.

"Willa? Did you hear me?"

Her hand trembled slightly and she clutched the phone even tighter as anger conquered her shame. She had a sudden idea. She glanced quickly at Nick, trying to remember if she'd referred to Eric by name. No, she hadn't. "Yes, I heard you. You're right," she said, avoiding the concerned look on Nick's face. "Maybe we should talk." She quickly agreed to meet him for dinner after work the next evening and said a fast good-bye before she lost her nerve.

As she looked back at Nick, her doubts increased. His gaze was too perceptive and she escaped it by turning her attention back to her schedule. Then she realized that if her plan worked, it solved the problem of having to deal with Nick as a client. Hoping she was doing the right thing, she picked up the pencil and made a few marks in her column before looking at him.

"I'm sorry we were interrupted," she stated, pleased at her calm, businesslike tone. "Monday at eleven will be fine, Mr. Logan."

TWO

It had been a long day after a sleepless night spent going over every aspect of her involvement with Eric. Willa had tried to convince herself that her judgment had been clouded by the stress of the heavy class load she'd undertaken in her push to get her second degree. She hadn't been very successful. And then there were Nick's suspicions that Doc had had something to do with switching drug-test results. The very idea was ludicrous. Not only had Doc helped her father through his long, arduous battle against cancer, but he'd gone out of his way to help her deal with the death of her father. She considered him family. No. No way would Doc compromise their relationship by knowingly allowing Eric to use her as a go-between.

Willa stood up and stretched, only to lean

forward and hold on to her desk as a wave of dizziness washed over her. When her head had cleared she glanced at her watch. Six-thirty. The day she thought would drag on forever had, in fact, zoomed by. She'd been so busy that she'd forgotten to have lunch. She knew she was asking for trouble skipping meals, but it was too late now. Soon she'd be meeting Eric for dinner. Still, she needed something. Hot tea, perhaps. With a healthy drop of honey.

As she left her office her thoughts were on her meeting with Eric. She refused to think of it as a date. She'd have to be very careful how she went about questioning him. Eric had been a two-timing, egotistical jerk, but to do what he'd been accused of, he'd also have to be ruthless . . . and cunning.

Willa's pace quickened as she headed up the curved staircase toward the reception area behind which was a small kitchen where the staff made tea and coffee. She turned at the top of the stairs and ran smack dab into six feet four inches of very determined male.

"Nick! What are you doing here? Are you meeting Sky?"

Nick took a brief second to enjoy her flustered response to his surprise visit. He told himself the warm feeling coursing through him was because his idea to catch her off guard had paid off better than he expected—not because he liked the sound of her smoky voice saying his name. "Actually I'm here for my first session. . . ." He purposely trailed off and shifted his gaze to the young woman behind the front desk.

Kelly, the receptionist, directed a nervous smile at Willa. "I'm sorry, Willa. I tried to tell you when you buzzed that your seven o'clock canceled. Uh, Mr. Logan asked to be notified if an opening came up before Monday. I didn't think you'd mind."

Kelly darted a quick look at Nick, and he felt his muscles tighten at her expression. She'd probably recognized him from all the media coverage after his arrest, and it was obvious she was uncomfortable. Nick tried to ignore the pain and the helpless anger that coursed through him, knowing he had no other choice. But he hated those looks. Part discomfort—as if he were some sort of dangerous criminal—part pity and disgust that such a promising athlete hadn't been strong enough to resist temptation.

He turned to Willa and forced a smile. "Yes, I hope you don't mind."

"Of course not," Willa answered quickly, wanting to ease the sudden tension in the room. She hadn't missed the tightening of Nick's jaw, making his smile more forced than natural, and wondered at the cause. Her stomach tightened again in a combination of hunger and stress, bringing her attention back to her reason for coming up in the first place. "But you are a bit early, and I have a few things to do before our session." She took several steps toward the archway leading to the kitchen. Motioning to the receptionist, she said, "I'm certain Kelly can start you on filling out the forms. I'll meet you in the training room in"—she glanced at her watch and grimaced—"fifteen minutes?"

"Sure. Take your time. I'm not going anywhere." Nick's smile broadened into a grin as she hurried from the room. Ms. Trask was obviously distracted about something, and it wasn't a last-minute change in her schedule. Funny. If he didn't know better, he'd swear her flustered response had as much to do with the way the atmosphere sizzled between them as any feelings of guilt she might be harboring.

He turned and caught Kelly's thoughtful expression and realized she hadn't missed the underlying tension between him and her boss. But he was surprised, and relieved, when she offered him a bright smile as she handed him the forms and a clipboard.

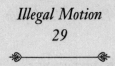

Willa ignored her stomach's rumble of protest as she went into the training room.

The room was almost deserted, not unusual around the dinner hour. She didn't see Nick. She scanned it again, but knew he wasn't among the men there. Even though he was wearing old white sweats and a light blue T-shirt, he'd still stand out in a group. She blew out a soft sigh of relief and sat down on one of the weight benches to begin filling out a training chart for him.

"Hi, sorry I'm a bit late. Those circular stairs are a bit tricky with the cane."

Willa jumped at the sound of his deep voice. The music piped into the room wasn't loud and there were no weights clanging around at the moment. So how did such a big guy—using a cane, no less—manage to move so quietly? "Have a seat." She gestured to the bench across from her.

She turned her attention back to the chart even though there wasn't much to fill in until she read his forms. But she was determined to stay cool and professional. Out of the corner of her eye she caught his quadriceps flexing as he sat down on the bench across from her. She quickly discovered several more lines that needed filling in.

"Do I make you nervous?"

Willa fought the flush rising to her cheeks. *Here it comes,* she thought, *he's getting ready to let me have it.* It was on the tip of her tongue to tell him everything, but his amused tone annoyed her. Besides, she reminded herself, the only thing she was really guilty of was being foolish enough to believe Eric had told the truth when he claimed to love her. "I just don't like people sneaking up on me, that's all," she explained. Looking directly at him, she reached for the forms he'd filled out, relieved that her hand was steady. The clipboard rested on his knee, but he made no move to hand it to her. Piqued by his attitude, she forced herself to maintain eye contact and refrained from snatching it off his knee.

"I'm sorry," he said quietly. "I'd forgotten how much you dislike being . . . distracted." The amused gleam in his eyes flashed brighter at the last word. He lifted the clipboard toward her, but she didn't take it, her eyes still on his. "Ms. Trask?" he prompted. "Willa?"

Hearing his deep voice saying her name so softly snapped her back to attention. She frowned as she took the forms, then forced a smile. *Think of him as a regular client,* she advised herself. But even looking at his bold handwriting bothered her, touching her as if he'd held the pen to her skin. *Get control of yourself, Willa. Keeping you off balance like this is exactly what he wants.* Pulling in several shallow breaths, she regained her control.

If he wanted a confession, then he was just going to have to come right out and ask her—she wasn't going to be a willing participant in any more of his seductive games.

She looked up at him, ready to begin the standard first workout interview, only to find his blue-eyed gaze running up and down her forest-green Millennium track suit. His slow scrutiny made her feel as though she'd dressed to display herself to him. Ridiculous considering she was covered head to toe in baggy nylon. But also disconcerting because the thought of dressing for his approval didn't seem the least bit repulsive to her. So much for reacting to him like an ordinary client. Nick Logan might be many things. Ordinary would never be one of them.

"So, where should we start? Do you want me standing up or lying down?"

Nick's deep voice broke into her thoughts like a velvet hammer. He obviously wasn't going to let up on her and she considered confronting him right then and there, putting an end to this charade. But she knew she'd have a far better chance of convincing him of her story if she had some facts from Eric to back it up. She glanced at her watch. Less than an hour to go. Certainly she could manage him for that long.

"Sitting will be fine, but I need to ask some questions first."

He smiled. "Shoot. My life is an open book."

There was a trace of bitterness in that last statement, and for the first time she thought about what his life must have been like these last eight months. She knew from the experience with her father how the media could insinuate themselves into every nook and cranny of your life until you'd do anything to get them off your back. It surprised her how badly she wanted to ask him about it, but just the knowledge that they shared a common bond gave her more confidence, and she smiled as she asked her first question.

"How long has it been since the last surgery on your knee?"

"Three weeks. So you're training pro football's fair-haired boy wonder."

Her smile faltered. He really had distraction down to a science. Getting a firm grip on the clipboard and her patience, she pretended not to know what he was talking about. "Who do you mean?"

"Your receptionist mentioned that Eric Miller was training here. She must have recognized me from when I played for the Jaguars and thought I might be interested."

Willa wanted to tell him to quit the games, that she knew exactly when he'd learned about Eric training here, but then she'd have to admit to overhearing his conversation with Sky. And that would lead to questions she wasn't ready to answer until later. "Actually I haven't seen him yet. He starts Monday."

"I got the impression from Kelly that you two were old acquaintances."

"Does every woman you come into contact with feel compelled to spill her guts?" Willa grumbled under her breath. But she knew Kelly was usually very professional, and his tactics only served to remind her what he was trying to do.

"Sorry, I didn't quite catch that."

She smiled stiffly. "I don't make a habit of discussing my private life, but if you must know, Eric and I dated a year or so ago. Now he's only a client."

"I'm surprised we never met, Willa. Not that I socialized with Eric much, but he did come to a barbecue I held for the camp kids. It would have been right about the time you dated. About eight months ago?"

Willa knew exactly what day he'd had the barbecue. It was the day she'd discovered Eric with one of the team's cheerleaders. She'd been so upset, she'd forgotten all about the host. Knowing he hadn't brought the subject up idly, she carefully steered the conversation away from the event.

"Camp kids? Sounds interesting, but I don't remember Eric ever mentioning anything about a camp." That was true. All she'd known was that it was the first team event he'd ever asked her to attend. Willa was surprised at the look of pain and defeat that crossed Nick's face. The sympathy she'd felt minutes ago returned. Obviously these kids had meant something to him.

"I—ah, that is, the Jaguars ran a summer camp every year during the off-season for some of the less privileged kids. Mostly from downtown Washington. I helped out a bit."

She knew from his expression that he'd done far more than help a bit. Intrigued by this side of him, she completely forgot the forms in her lap. "I take it the players gave seminars and stuff at the camp?"

"Some did. Others stayed for a few weeks at a time as counselors. You'd be amazed at how important it is to a young kid to have someone to look up to."

"Someone like you? You were one of the counselors, weren't you?"

"Yeah. I used to be." Nick hated the shame and humiliation that coursed through him every time he thought of how he'd let those kids down. Dammit, it wasn't even his fault. And that alone was the main reason he'd do anything to clear his name. He sensed Willa's sensitivity to this subject and it confused him. He wanted to think she was guilty as sin. It was much easier to go about gathering evidence when he didn't have to deal with his growing suspicion that the woman he'd thought partially responsible might be as innocent a victim as he.

He put that thought aside, still frustrated that she'd neatly turned the tables on him. He didn't like it that she'd so easily gotten him to discuss a subject even Sky knew better than to bring up. Never mind that he'd been the one to mention the camp kids in the first place.

"I thought you wanted to know more about my knee injury."

Her sympathetic expression faltered at his terse statement, and he was relieved when she gamely switched gears.

Glancing back at her clipboard, as if the interview hadn't gone off topic, she asked, "Tell me more about the exact nature of your knee injury. How it happened, that sort of thing. Was this a football injury?"

You know damn well it wasn't a football injury, he wanted to shout. *Damn her control.* "No, I didn't play last season." He tried hard to keep his tone casual, but doubted he'd succeeded. "I tripped over a cord about a month ago and wrenched it pretty badly, tore some ligaments."

Her expression now was purely professional, and for some reason that irritated the hell out of him. "I'm sorry if I got too personal earlier. Guess ol' Eric is a sore spot, huh? Guess I shouldn't have brought him up. Must have hurt like hell when he dumped you."

Willa blanched. Familiar emotions like pain and humiliation welled up whenever she thought about her relationship with Eric. But now she also felt angry, and for the first time she defended herself. "He didn't dump me, Nick," she snapped, wanting to wipe that smug look off of his face. "*I* dumped *him.* The lousy slimeball was two-timing me. Hell, he was probably three-timing me!"

"Honest mistake." His tone was anything but contrite. "As I said, I didn't hang around with Eric much, but I know his reputation with women. He wasn't exactly known as the kind of guy who was ready to make anything resembling a commitment. Far from it. He was notorious for leaving women when they got too close. So I just assumed . . ." Nick trailed off as he noticed her expression change. His taunt had produced a look of gut-deep pain.

Nick was on intimate terms with the kind of personal demons it took to feel that kind of pain—and nothing could have forced him to put her through any more at the moment. "I'm sorry, Willa. You're right, what happened between you and Eric is none of my business." But he wanted it to be. And not because he thought it would give him more ammunition for his case against Miller, but because he wanted to help her deal with and get over whatever the bastard had done to her.

And that scared the daylights out of him.

Willa didn't know what to think. She felt foolish for letting him goad her into that outburst. She eyed him warily, but judging from his expression, his last comment had been completely sincere. For the life of her she didn't know why, though. Wasn't this what he wanted? For her to lose control and reveal the truth?

She'd only been alone with Nick for a few minutes and he'd already irritated her, embarrassed her, made her lose her temper again—and now, amazingly enough, he seemed to be trying to comfort her. "I'm the one who's sorry," she said. A tentative smile touched her lips. "You seem to bring out the unprofessional in me."

His responding grin created a small glow inside of her. *He should smile more often*, she thought. *Those pearly whites are almost as devastating as his baby blues*. If she wasn't careful she might start to care about him—really care.

"We'd better concentrate our time on setting up your program. Tell me more about your injury."

"You probably won't believe this," Nick responded, his smile becoming somewhat sheepish, "but I was out jogging, and I tripped over a dog leash. At the time it was still attached to the dog."

His self-deprecating tone and boyish grin were both qualities she wouldn't have associated with him, and they were completely endearing. "And you twisted your knee when you fell?"

"Actually, aside from the trauma to an old knee injury, there was also a shoulder separation."

She could have sworn his face was actually reddening. Her voice hovering on laughter, she asked, "Your shoulder or the dog's? And what kind of dog was it anyway, a Great Dane?"

"Ah, the dog wasn't hurt." Nick mumbled something else that Willa couldn't hear.

He was blushing! "I'm sorry, what kind of dog did you say it was?"

"I don't see what difference it makes, but it was a poodle. A toy poodle."

Smiling broadly now, but still struggling to keep from laughing out loud, she said, "I assume then that these injuries weren't sustained in self-defense."

"I'll have you know," Nick shot back indignantly, "that the little black-haired rat actually bit me while I was lying there, writhing in pain! I'm flat out on the path, my knee and my shoulder are on fire, and the little bugger bit me right on the— Never mind."

Willa sobered immediately. Vivid pictures came to mind of the part of his anatomy most likely to have sustained the bite.

When Nick raised his eyebrow in her line of vision, she cleared her throat and looked away. The old kiss-it-and-make-it-better remedy had never had such erotic overtones.

"Willa?" Nick's quiet tone dragged her gaze up to his eyes. "Will you help me?"

In that instant she knew. *He knows that I know why he's here.* He wasn't just asking her to help heal his body. He was asking her to heal his soul.

Willa wasn't sure if she was willing to risk giving him what he so desperately needed, but in that moment she realized she had to try. Despite their constant sparring matches, which, she had to admit, she found strangely stimulating, she found it was getting harder to deny her growing attraction to this very determined, very sexy man.

"I'll do what I can, Nick." She had taken the safe way out, not wanting to be the first to broach the real subject at hand. She only hoped he realized the true meaning behind her carefully chosen answer.

"That's all I can ask. And I like it when you call me Nick."

"Hello, I thought I might find you here."

Willa looked up at the man she'd hoped never to see again. Before she could come up with a response, Nick turned to greet his former teammate. She stiffened, her gaze riveted to the look that passed between them.

"Eric Miller. I haven't seen you in—oh . . . almost a year now." Nick's smile made it no further than his lips; his eye remained an icy shade of blue.

"Logan, how's it going? Why the cane? Hurt yourself coaching a peewee team or something?"

"Or something." Nick spoke quietly, his tone lethal. Looking pointedly at his watch, he then turned to Willa and said, "I'll start on some of the stretches my doctor recommended before we start your program." Willa nodded in response, and Nick lifted his cane and moved off to the other side of the training area without another word to Eric.

Eric walked over and dropped his shiny multi-pocketed gym bag next to Nick's old, cracked leather one. Willa barely waited for him to turn back to her before speaking.

"What are you doing here? I thought we weren't supposed to meet until eight-thirty?"

Looking put out, he responded in a coaxing tone. "I'd tell you that I came early to use the whirlpool, but the truth is, I couldn't wait to see you. So I decided to check if I could persuade you to play hooky and leave early."

She hadn't laid eyes on him since the day she'd walked into his apartment and discovered him locked in more than a passionate embrace on the living-room floor with a very healthy, very naked blonde.

And he had the nerve to say he couldn't wait another hour to see her again! Willa felt the rolling tide of her stomach pitch violently toward her throat. Had she really been that taken in by the golden-boy charm and practiced pout? The humiliating answer was yes. But she knew better now—now it made her sick. "I'm sorry, Eric. But as you can see, I have a client to train—"

"Yeah, right. What in the hell is that has-been cokehead doing here?"

If she'd been a man, she'd have punched him right in the face. Even so, she felt her fingers curling into fists. "Nick is a client," she said through gritted teeth. "If you intend to wait for me, why don't you go on up to the lounge?"

"I'd rather wait in your office. You know, with people coming in and out, I'd be stuck signing autographs and stuff. I'd appreciate the privacy."

Willa refrained from rolling her eyes and capitulated. Anything to get him out of this room. "Fine, it's down the hall to the left. But it will be at least another hour."

"All right, I guess you're worth it." Eric smiled and tilted his head toward her.

Shocked by his audacity, Willa froze. Only a loud clanging from the other side of the gym kept Eric from kissing her.

"Sorry." Nick's low voice carried easily across the gym, his tone anything but sincere. "Boy, these plates are heavy," he added as he turned back to the machine he'd been loading up with the huge, black iron disks.

Willa had jumped a foot away from Eric when Nick "accidentally" dropped the plate. She felt like winking at him for his timely intervention.

Nick was glad that his instincts had taken over and kept Willa and Eric apart, but he cursed himself for having to admit that his reasons went way beyond clearing his name.

Scowling, he piled two more plates on the quad machine and began a punishing set of leg extensions.

Willa scooped up Nick's leather bag and headed across the room. As soon as she realized what he was doing, her professionalism took over. She dropped his bag and the clipboards and forcibly stopped him from doing another repetition. "What in the hell are you trying to do? Set your orthopedic surgeon up in a life of luxury?"

"Actually," he responded, surprised at how easy it was to grin, "he's already paid off the car. Maybe this will help with the yacht loan."

"Not funny, Logan." Thoroughly confused, she still had to fight the urge to respond to his teasing grin. She could have sworn he was angry at her when he'd left her with Eric. "You said you came to me because I'm the best. Well, I am. And if you want my help, we're going to do this my way. Got it?"

Nick took in her flushed skin and bright green eyes. "Oh yeah, I got it." His voice softened, all traces of joking gone. *And I think I got it real bad.* Even though there were still a few people left in the training room, his focus narrowed down to just the two of them. For all he knew they were in a vacuum. He couldn't hear anything except the pounding in his chest, could only feel a sudden throbbing—and it was nowhere near the region of his knee.

"I think we should start with something that puts a little less direct pressure on the knee."

What did she say . . . pressure? Knee? "I was using my right knee."

"What?" Willa looked down at his legs and realized he'd only been lifting with his healthy knee. "Oh, well, I still wish you'd waited for me." Feeling somewhat foolish over her outburst, Willa moved over to a flat bench. "Why don't we start with some easy stretches so I can see what kind of mobility you have. After we've gone through those, it will be easier to decide what machines you should start on."

Nick slid off the narrow seat of the leg-extension machine and hopped over to the flat bench. He took a moment to watch Willa, her expression so serious as she jotted some notes a bit too furiously on the page. Telling himself he was just following his plan by teasing her, he turned and lay back on the bench, propping his feet up on the other end. Pillowing his head on his crossed arms, he said, "I always knew we'd start out lying down."

Either the stress of the afternoon had gotten

to her or the lack of food—likely both—but she couldn't keep from responding in kind. "Don't get too excited, Logan, only one of us is going to be horizontal."

Nick breathed a sigh of what sounded like deep satisfaction. "Yeah, that's one of my favorite positions too."

For the first time in her career, her life, Willa completely lost control and whacked Nick's rock-hard abdomen with her clipboard. At his shocked expression, her broad smile dissolved into giggles, which ended with her collapsing on the floor next to him, clutching her middle as his laughter blended with hers.

She was having way too much fun with him. She was light-headed. She should have taken time for lunch. Lunch reminded her of dinner and that brought her full circle to Eric and Nick's real reason for being with her in the first place. Her laughter faded and she abruptly looked at the clock. Time was running out. Soon she'd have to face Eric.

Frowning now, she wasn't sure which bothered her most, having to leave when it looked as if she might get Nick to trust her enough to listen. Or having to face Eric again. Willa rubbed her temples to alleviate a sudden pounding.

Nick was watching her intently. He'd been

completely captivated by her deep, husky laugh, and more than a little pleased to have been the reason for it. He realized that he'd truly relaxed for the first time since Eric had left.

Was that what brought a frown to her face? That she'd been enjoying his company? Was she afraid Eric would be jealous? Or maybe she didn't want to see Eric. Just wishful thinking on his part? Either way, it was a sure bet that Eric Miller wanted to see Willa. And from the looks Miller had given her when he hadn't been occupied with looking at himself in the mirrors, Nick would say the boy wonder had a lot more than business on his mind.

"What's wrong? Is our time up already?" Nick asked.

"Nothing's wrong. I'm just—"

"Not used to having fun with your clients?" Willa's quick flash of guilt was as soothing to his wounded pride as it was intriguing. Had Eric, or someone else, hurt her so badly that she was afraid to loosen up?

"Actually we have enough time to go through the stretches," she said, quickly scooping up the clipboard, then rising onto her knees beside him. "After tonight I'll work up a routine for you. You'll need to set up your first few workouts so I can supervise them and make any necessary changes. After that, any of the people here on staff will be able to help you."

Willa smiled in relief when Nick seemed to accept their return to business. His last taunt had hit too close to home. She put down her clipboard and positioned herself next to his legs. She reached out, intending to bend his bad knee, but stopped just short of actually touching the nicely filled-out white sweats. Suddenly the idea of touching him took on wholly unprofessional dimensions.

"It's the left knee."

Nick's voice was strained as if he were in pain. But she hadn't done anything yet. Focusing on the knee and not the man it belonged to, she gently gripped his leg, one hand under his thigh, the other on his calf. It was like touching granite. She paused for a moment, her fingers flexing together as she grappled with the sensations racing through her. Nick remained perfectly still—too still—and she looked up to see his jaw tighten into a grimace.

Before she could ask him if he was hurt, he abruptly sat up.

"Did I hurt you?" she asked quickly. "Are you in pain?"

"Yeah, you might say that." Nick let out a short laugh. "Listen, I know we have a few minutes left. But I can tell you're in a hurry to get out of here, so why don't we finish this some other time? I still have my Monday appointment, so we can do this then." Maybe by Monday his sweats wouldn't tent like a teenager with his first crush every time she touched him.

Willa didn't know what had happened, but she was coward enough to take his suggestion. In the past few hours her feelings toward Nick Logan had gone through as many ups and downs as if she'd been on an emotional roller coaster.

"Monday sounds fine," she answered, hurrying to collect the training files and clipboards. She was halfway to the door when he caught up with her and stopped her by placing his hand on the door over her shoulder.

He was so close that Willa could smell his skin. The faint musky scent invaded her nostrils and she wondered distractedly if a taste of him would adequately make up for the meals she'd missed today. Dangerous thoughts. She swallowed in a vain attempt to moisten her throat. He was so close. They were eye to eye—or rather eye to lips.

"Who has got you in such a panic, Willa? I hope it's not me. I'm harmless." Proving he was anything but, he shifted his weight forward until their bodies were almost touching. "That means it must be your date this evening. That's a real shame, Willa. I think a man should keep his woman quivering in anticipation." His gaze fastened on her trembling lower lip. "Not shaking in her shoes."

THREE

His woman . . . quivering. Willa gasped, her lips parting slightly.

That did it. Nick lost the tenuous hold on his control and gave in to the urge to touch her. Lifting his hand, he toyed first with a wisp of her hair. Her eyes dilated at his brief touch and he continued, running his fingertip across her lower lip and wondering what it would taste like. He knew he had to stop, and even started to move back when she lifted her hand. His good intentions went up in smoke when she ran her finger lightly over the scrape of beard along his jawline.

"You know, you should smile more often," she said, the return of the husky edge to her voice driving him crazy.

"I haven't had much to smile about lately," he answered honestly, then sucked in his breath when her finger brushed his lower lip. "Willa, I—"

A loud gurgling sound interrupted him and Willa jumped away from him as if coming out of a trance. Flustered, she looked around, wondering what had made that noise. When the sound repeated itself, her expression turned to one of mortification.

Although he was not sure whether he should be frustrated or relieved at the interruption, the cause nevertheless made him smile. "Gee, I sure hope this guy plans on feeding you." Her skin darkened further and he gave in to the urge to soothe her embarrassment. Placing a finger under her chin, he gently turned her face back to his. "Just promise me you'll order something big and expensive. Deal?" His efforts earned him a smile and a nod. It made him want to kiss her, to tell her that Eric Miller was a bastard and demand that she cancel their date and— "Good night, Willa," he said abruptly, his voice still hoarse. He leaned down to scoop up the cane he'd dropped during their heated exchange and walked back across the now deserted room to get his gym bag.

Willa clasped the clipboard to her chest and pushed through the door. Once in the hall, she leaned against the wall and took in several deep breaths. It didn't help. Without a doubt she was in over her head. Way over her head.

She hurried toward her office before Nick could come out and find her still standing there. Eric was waiting in her office. She had to be clearheaded if she was going to pull this off.

Willa wasn't sure if she had any willpower left to deal with Eric and this whole mess tonight. What she really wanted was to go home and sink into a tub full of steaming water, drink a glass of chilled wine, and pretend the past two days had never happened. Then she thought of Nick, and how for a moment he'd seemed to look into her soul and request her help in healing his. She couldn't ignore that, or her responsibility to him. Whatever his motives were for the little scene in the doorway, she still needed to clear his name. And her own.

She was a fool if she thought for one minute that he had any real desire for her. He believed she had betrayed him, cost him a part of his life. Even if she exonerated herself, there was no way he could ever look at her without being reminded of his past and her significant role in it. And for that she couldn't blame him. She had to clear him *and* stay clear of him.

Eric straightened immediately from behind her desk as she entered the room. Before Willa could question him on what he was doing, he asked her a question.

"Where have you been? I feel like I've been waiting for hours." His pout made Willa sick.

Swallowing her distaste, she said, "Sorry I'm late, Eric. My last appointment ran a little long."

"Well, are you ready to go?" Eric jammed his hand through his salon-styled blond hair and shifted from one foot to the other. He seemed impatient, almost edgy.

"I still have to shower and help Kelly lock up. It will only take about thirty minutes, but if you'd rather not—"

"No, that's okay." Eric walked toward her, looking contrite over his less than polite greeting. "I'm sorry, Willa, I guess I'm just anxious to be alone with you."

He touched her arm, and she casually moved away. "Why don't you go ahead to the restaurant and order our drinks," she said, her voice bright. *And about ten appetizers*, she added silently. "I'll meet you there."

"That's okay. I'll wait here."

She hadn't forgotten he'd been behind her desk when she'd come in and she wasn't about to leave him in her office alone again. "Why don't you wait upstairs in the reception-area lounge?

It's closing time, so I don't think you'll be bothered."

"I'll be counting the minutes." Eric flashed his perfect teeth. "I'm really glad to be seeing you again."

As he bent his head closer Willa reached behind her and opened the door. "The sooner I leave, the sooner I'll be back." She backed through the doorway and pointed up the hallway. "Just head up those stairs and take a right."

Eric had no choice but to leave the office. Willa locked the door and headed the opposite way down the hall.

Twenty minutes later she emerged from the locker room, showered and changed, though not exactly refreshed. Pulling her hair into a pony-tail, she fixed it with one of her favorite green puffy bands. She adjusted a thin leather belt over a forest-green print shirt. She couldn't stop her thoughts from wandering to Nick and imagining what it would be like to dress for him, to see his blue eyes light up in admiration. Her smile broadened as she recalled the way his gaze had all but devoured her in her green track suit. She was sure Nick would like her to dress down—preferably completely.

The idea of undressing for him was undeniably tantalizing, especially since it would only happen in the safe confines of her imagination. Enchanted by the idea of working through her distraction with Nick by playing out their earlier scene to a more satisfying, and perfectly private, conclusion, she let her thoughts drift.

Sensuous images filled her head, startling her with their intensity, but she willingly followed their lead. After all, she reasoned, the stronger the medicine, the better the cure. After a moment or two a new sensation skittered over her heated skin, but it was slow to overpower the other, increasingly erotic ones. It took her a long moment to realize the tingling awareness was trying to tell her she was no longer alone.

Embarrassed at being caught fantasizing, absurdly feeling as if her erotic thoughts were displayed over her head in a cartoonlike bubble, she looked around in what she hoped was a nonchalant manner. She didn't pull it off.

Leaning against the wall, a self-assured smile spreading lazily over his face and erasing any doubt about how long he'd been standing there, was Nick.

She tried to blame it on her steamy musings, but he seemed even sexier than before. His fresh-from-the-shower appeal only served to strengthen the energy that seemed to radiate from him. It certainly energized her. She took in his appearance all at once, and it was like grabbing a hot wire. His faded, snug jeans proved her guesses about his well-developed thighs had been correct. She noticed that his knee wasn't—couldn't be—bandaged any longer. *What else wasn't he wearing under those jeans?*

Realizing she was gawking, she returned her gaze to his face—which sent her already electrified system sizzling into overload. His wet black hair was curlier now, the longer strands in the back clinging to his bared neck. Her gaze helplessly tracked the tiny beads of water as they trickled off the ends of his curls, slowly sliding down the side of his jaw.

His low chuckle made her vibrate. She fought the absurd desire to look over his head to see if his thoughts were conveniently on display, as moments ago she had felt hers were.

Feeling silly and defenseless, but mostly embarrassed at being caught in such a vulnerable state, she had a sudden, desperate need to wipe the smirk off his face. So it was to her horror that she blurted out, "Don't you own anything that doesn't fit you like a second skin?" That remark only served to broaden his grin to downright lethal proportions, and she quickly added, "You, uh, you took a long time getting dressed. You do know we close soon?"

"Would you believe I lost track of time while I was fantasizing about you in the sauna?" Nick's smile broadened wickedly when her blush deepened to a fiery scarlet. "Picture it. There I am, all relaxed, when I feel a slight draft. I look up, and you're standing in front of me, wearing one of those thick club towels. One corner is tucked snugly above your breast."

His seductive words were spoken in that velvety voice. In the back of her mind, she was perversely irritated at how much better his fantasy was than hers. His low groan roused her like a douse of cold water. Not trusting herself to speak, she looked away, snapping the sensual web he was expertly weaving, and stalked past him toward the stairs. At that moment she didn't care if he followed her or stayed the night.

She stopped just outside the door to the reception area and took a deep, calming breath. Pressing her hands to her cheeks, she willed them to cool off, hoping Eric attributed her flushed skin to a hot shower. She pushed through the door, letting it swing shut behind her.

She didn't pay attention to the soft thud as the door connected with Nick's toe, or the colorful string of curses that followed. Her mind was focused solely on collecting her so-called date and getting the hell out of there before something else happened. Kelly could deal with that dream-weaving devil.

She didn't stop to consider that she would be spending the next several hours of her life valiantly trying to clear that devil's good name. Not to mention her own.

Willa found Eric bending low over the counter, facing in the other direction. He had apparently put his charm to use, as Kelly was gone and the place was already locked up. Too rattled to pay attention to what he was doing now, just wanting to leave, she pasted on a bright smile and said in an overly cheerful rush, "Eric, there you are. Sorry I kept you waiting."

Nick heard Willa's animated greeting and scowled. He recalled in perfect detail her very expressive face during his improvised sauna scenario. He thought about how much he'd enjoy spending the rest of the night finding out if her body could be as delightfully aroused as her mind. Then he remembered that her body and her mind would be spending the rest of the evening, and possibly the night, with Eric Miller.

Nick felt as if he had just been tackled and left strangely out of sync at a time when he desperately needed to rely on his instincts. Something about her date with Eric made him uneasy. Whatever she was up to, she was in over her head. He'd hung around hoping he could find out why Miller had been so keen to be alone in Willa's office, but the door had been locked. So he told himself once again that his decision to follow them on her date was in his best interests and had nothing to do with any protective feelings he might have for Willa.

Nick pushed through the door. "Hope I'm not interrupting any business." Willa's jolt at his inflection on that last word told him his instincts might be right this time. "Forget about me, Willa?" The implication that she'd forgotten him once before was clear, and her skin faded a bit more. The expression on her face should have kept his anger firmly in place; instead he felt like a louse for adding to her obvious distress.

"Logan, what are you still doing here?" Eric's tone made it clear he suspected Willa's late arrival might have something to do with Nick.

"That seems to be the popular question this evening." Nick moved slowly toward the door, his unbandaged knee making him lean heavily on the cane. "The fact is, I'd like to leave this den of hospitality, if someone wouldn't mind unlocking the door."

"Since everyone else is gone, why don't we all leave together? Eric, are you coming?"

Nick moved to open the door, but was almost trampled as Eric hurried to get there first. He caught Willa rolling her eyes at Miller's macho "I'm her date, I'll get the door" theatrics and couldn't resist temptation. A grin split his face as he casually stuck out his cane in a standing-ovation variety of "no, let me" comebacks. When Eric stumbled, Nick pressed his advantage and leaned on the door so that Eric went sailing right on out before recovering his balance. Nick turned to Willa in time to catch the grin on her face before she smoothed it into a reproachful glare.

Still, her lips twitched when Nick gave her a courtly bow and very calmly said, "After you, madam."

As she passed through the door Nick let his gaze travel over Willa's khaki-covered backside as his hand slid down the glass door to the handle. He carefully pressed the button to prevent the door from locking automatically and hoped Willa and Eric would make an early night of it.

Now that the time had come to put her plan in motion, Willa began to have serious doubts. "Do you need a ride?" she asked Nick, not caring at this point what meaning he might read into her request.

"No, thanks. Gave up my stick shift and leased an automatic after my knee surgery. Other than looking a bit awkward getting in and out, it's no problem."

Nick bent down and grabbed his old leather bag that he'd dropped while holding the door. Willa found her gaze drawn to the fluid motion of flexing muscle as he bent over. The athletic grace of his huge body was breathtaking, and she couldn't imagine him being awkward at much of anything.

After Nick waved them off, Eric shepherded Willa toward his Porsche. It looked sinister somehow; an icy glow seemed to emanate from the glossy black finish as the rising moon caressed its sleek curves with an otherworldly light. An uncontrollable shiver slithered down her spine.

Willa quickly decided she needed space and some time to get her act together before facing the evening ahead. She ducked out from under his arm.

"Why don't I meet you at the restaurant?" Forestalling his objection, she continued, "I hate leaving my car in an empty lot. I know it's nothing fancy," she said, gesturing to her small red Honda, "but it's all I've got."

She waved and turned away, pretending not to notice his disgruntled expression. It took all of her willpower not to run to her car and lock herself inside.

Eric left the table for at least the third time since they'd arrived. Willa stifled a yawn and toyed with the stem of her wineglass. Reviewing the evening, she came to the only conclusion possible: Mata Hari she wasn't. Eric had been so busy ranting and raving about his unfair treatment by the Jaguars coaching staff this season that she hadn't gotten a word in. Eric had always been self-centered, but tonight he'd seemed almost paranoid.

Too tired to analyze that thought, she glanced again at the archway leading to the front of the restaurant and the rest rooms. She debated taking another sip of the outrageously costly wine she'd insisted Eric order—smiling as she recalled Nick's request that she order something big and expensive—but shrugged instead and pushed to her feet. She swayed a bit and paused to get her bearings. She wasn't drunk; she'd barely finished one glass of wine, but her plan to order entrée after expensive entrée had died on the first whiff of seafood. It was one of her favorite things to eat, so she figured it must be the company that made her stomach churn.

Stifling a yawn, she headed to the front of the restaurant, not caring what the hostess thought about her leaving without her date. She barely suppressed a giggle as it occurred to her that Eric probably wouldn't even notice she'd left.

"Willa? Where are you going?"

Damn. Almost made it. Taking a deep breath, she turned to face Eric. "I'm sorry, Eric, but it's late and I'm very tired. You kept disappearing, so I just thought . . ." She purposely trailed off, hoping he'd pick up on her light accusation and take the defensive position for a change.

"Oh. Yeah. Sorry about that." His frown faded quickly, though, and he added, "Let me take care of the bill and I'll be right back."

Willa nodded tiredly and leaned against the wall.

Eric reappeared minutes later. "Sorry, the waitress took forever."

It occurred to her that Eric always managed to put the blame on someone else, but had little time to ponder that thought as he threw his arm around her shoulder and ushered her out the door. Caught off guard, Willa stumbled along, unable to get her balance long enough to shrug off his unwanted embrace.

Steering her toward his car, he asked, "Are you up for some dancing? Or maybe a drink? Someplace private."

Willa didn't try to hide her amazement at his total lack of regard for her very obvious fatigue. He hadn't even noticed that she drank dinner. She all but snorted in disgust.

At a complete loss for words, she remained silent until he opened his passenger door, gestured her inside, and asked, "Where do you want to go first?"

"Eric, I'm sorry, but it's been a really long day. I really have to head home." Willa tried to duck back out from under his arm.

Miffed at her refusal, Eric rebounded quickly, flashing that cereal-box grin as he tightened his hold on her, preventing her escape. "When will I see you again?"

Her acting ability long since depleted, she managed a weak smile while she struggled for the right words—ones that would get him to leave as quickly as possible without destroying her hopes of getting information out of him later.

Eric, interpreting her pause as a refusal to go out with him again, veered sharply from the polite cereal-ad athlete to the spoiled star used to people granting his every whim. "What is it, Willa? I'm not good enough for you now?"

He turned suddenly, pinning her loosely between his body and his car. Willa was a little surprised by his mercurial mood swing, but didn't think he meant her any real harm.

"Is there someone else? Logan, maybe?" Eric leaned a little closer. Whatever he saw in Willa's eyes seemed to confirm his suspicions. "I should have suspected something was up when you two were so late coming upstairs."

Alarm signals began going off in her tired brain. Now that he'd moved closer, she could see the unnatural brightness in his eyes. The depth of her stupidity would have shamed her if she hadn't been so frightened. How could she have missed it? His many trips to the men's room, his strange mood swings, his paranoia . . . Nick was right, Eric was using drugs. Heavily, if tonight was any indication. She suddenly recalled how she'd found him bent over the reception desk earlier. Had he been snorting cocaine right in the club? She had to get away from Eric.

It took all of her remaining willpower, but she managed to force her features into what she hoped was a calm mask. "I only met Mr. Logan yesterday. I'm just his trainer." She wondered if she sounded convincing. "I went out with you because you wanted us to act like adults and be friends."

Her emphasis on the word "friends" had the opposite effect than the one she'd hoped for. He shocked her by pulling her roughly against him.

"Friends, huh?" he ground out. "I'll show you friends." He bent his head as if he meant to kiss her, but stopped a mere inch from her face, his pupils dilated. "You may have been the naive little virgin, but we both know that isn't the case anymore, don't we, Willa?"

Initially frozen by his surprising move, Willa managed to gather her wits as he lowered his face the last inch. She wrenched to her left while pushing at his chest. Eric wasn't prepared for her sudden move and stumbled back, letting go of her.

Trembling, she wrapped her arms around her waist. "I think that you should leave." Eric sobered a bit at her quiet request, but when he took a step toward her, she raised a hand. "Now. Good night, Eric."

Eric swore at her as he slammed the passenger door shut and stormed to the other side. Willa closed her mind to his ugly words, barely turning in time to avoid the spray of gravel when he gunned the powerful engine and squealed out of the parking lot.

Gulping in air, Willa leaned weakly on her car. She purposely shut out all of the emotions threatening to swamp her in the aftermath of the near violence she'd just experienced. She hugged herself tightly, but couldn't seem to stop shaking. That, combined with exhaustion and the wine she had consumed on a daylong empty stomach was her excuse when she began to giggle. Ignoring the slightly hysterical edge, she said, "This spy stuff sure isn't as easy as it looks on TV," then promptly fainted on the hood of her car.

Nick reached her before she hit the ground.

FOUR

Nick pulled Willa's limp form against his body, turning her so he could scoop her up into his arms. His knee protested strongly as he hobbled back across the pavement.

"Not exactly a lightweight, are you?" he murmured against her hair, which smelled like cigarette smoke now. He preferred the elusive scent he'd noticed at the club. Long and lean, her muscled body was heavy, making his knee burn as if someone had pushed a hot needle into it. Still, he held her close—his concern for her more important than damaging his knee.

Her breathing evened, and although she looked pale in the glow of the parking-area lamplight, Nick was fairly certain she was sleeping. "Lady, what you do to me . . ." Nick kept his voice, husky from strain, low and close to her ear.

"My brain is telling me I have every reason to mistrust you," he said, and groaned as she snuggled closer when he shifted her to open the door. Her firm backside now rested against the front of his jeans. "Of course, certain fibers of my being disagree with that judgment."

Willa shifted slightly, vaguely aware of feeling comforted. Her muzzy brain registered the fact that she was being held in someone's arms. She struggled briefly, thinking Eric had come back, but when she heard Nick's deep voice in her ear, she relaxed, certain that she must be home, safe in bed, giving full rein to the fantasy she'd started outside the locker room earlier. She turned and snuggled deeper into her bed. After the day she had, she deserved to enjoy whatever harmless fun her mind conjured up.

If she wiggled against him one more time, Nick didn't think he'd make it to the car. He sighed in relief as he reached the sedan and placed her on the leather seat as gently as he could. *Damn knee.* He leaned in and pulled the tiny lever that released the seat, holding it until it reclined fully. To do this, he practically had to lie on top of her. He started to pull away, but couldn't resist brushing the loosened tendrils of hair from her face. His fingers lingered on the edge of her cheekbone and he found himself leaning toward her invitingly parted lips.

Suddenly realizing what he'd been about to do, he yanked his head back, bringing it squarely into contact with the overhead seat-belt hook. Swearing at newfangled cars and his close call, he quickly closed the door and limped around to his side. "I should've kept that damned bandage on," he grumbled. But no, like an idiot he'd taken it off because he hated Willa using the visual reminder of his weakness against him. And just maybe he wanted her to see him as whole and strong—not as an object of pity or scorn.

Nick couldn't remember the last time he'd tried to impress a woman by showing off. For that matter he couldn't remember ever wanting to.

He pulled over by her car to pick up her purse. Probably dropped it fending off that lecherous jerk. A jerk whose example he'd almost followed. *Worse*, he reminded himself, *at least she was conscious when Miller put his moves on her*. Uttering another string of oaths, he pulled himself out of the car and grabbed the small leather bag. After locking her doors, he levered himself back into the driver's seat and pulled out of the lot.

Nick divided his attention between the road and looking over at Willa. She had shifted positions several times, murmuring little contented noises as she burrowed into the plush cushions of the luxury car. He groaned and forced himself to focus on where he was going as he neared the rural area of eastern Loudoun County. He sent a silent thank-you to Sky for insisting that Nick know where she lived. He just hoped Willa didn't question him too closely. They had enough lies between them.

Nick tried to use the time the long drive provided to sort out his strange and conflicting feelings for her. But twenty minutes later he hadn't come up with any answers. Only more questions. Like why his gut had twisted so tightly when Miller had pulled her into his arms. Nick had been out of the car and halfway across the lot before it occurred to him that she might *want* to be there. So why had he been so proud of the way she'd handled the creep?

Nick glanced over at her again, as if her sleeping form would yield some answers, but his puzzled frown split into a wide grin when she started snoring lightly.

He turned onto the gravel drive, the moon providing the only light other than the car's high beams. He slowly made his way to the farmhouse at the end of the quarter-mile lane, wondering how she'd react when she found out who'd driven her home. He didn't have to wait long to find out. He'd avoided most of the holes in the rutted lane, but the car still bounced several times, finally waking her.

It took all of two seconds for Willa to realize she wasn't home in bed. Her gaze swung wildly from side to side; she was slow to comprehend the door handle and ashtray on one side, but easily recognized the silhouette of the man beside her. The same man she'd been dreaming about . . . That meant that he'd really carried her—

"What do you think you're doing?" she demanded as she lurched forward, grabbing onto the dashboard to keep from falling back onto the seat.

"Ah, the lovely princess has awakened. I see your temper doesn't improve with rest." At her glare, he continued, "What I think I'm doing is driving you home. This is the right address, isn't it? All these silos look the same in the dark." He opened his door and the interior light came on. He started to lean toward her, but stopped when she backed up against the door.

"Don't even think about it," she warned, eyeing him warily. "I've had enough of predatory males for one evening, thank you."

"Fine, have it your way. Still, you'd probably be more comfortable if you would let me put the seat up."

Her face flamed. "I'm sorry, I . . . It's been a hell of a day." She shook her head as if to clear the cobwebs, and the elastic band holding her hair slid off onto the seat.

Nick's gaze shifted to her hair, more gold than red in the dim overhead light, and watched it cascade around her shoulders. She looked like Sleeping Beauty must have looked just after being awakened.

Willa scrambled to get out of the car. While she fumbled with the high-tech lock on the door, Nick grabbed his cane and circled the car to her door. "It's unlocked," he said, but she didn't hear him through the glass. He pulled the door open and bent in to help her as she started to climb out. Their heads connected with an audible thud and Willa plopped back down on the seat.

Both of them were swearing now and rubbing their foreheads. "I don't know which is more dangerous," Nick said. "You or the car. And where in the world did you learn to swear like that?"

"My father tried his best to shield me from the baser aspects of sports, but when you spend your formative years around training facilities filled with professional athletes, you're bound to learn a few unusual phrases."

Nick chuckled, then winced as his hand found

the other knot forming on the back of his head. "Didn't know you could do that to a football."

"What happened tonight? Why are you here? Or should I say, why were you there?" Gingerly probing the sore spot on her forehead, she started to rephrase the vague question when Nick waved her silent.

Knowing that now was definitely not the time to tell her the real reason he had been conveniently available, he resorted to fabricating an answer. "Call it a strange coincidence, but I had stopped in at Bennigan's around the corner, and as I was leaving I got lost in the confusing maze of parking lots surrounding those office buildings." She looked skeptical, but hell, on a moment's notice, he thought it sounded pretty good. "Anyway, I was turning around in Devon's lot when I saw you leaning on your car. I pulled over to see if you needed help and you fainted dead away." *In my arms*, he wanted to add, but didn't.

Willa didn't feel like remembering, much less discussing, the events that had led up to the finale of her so-called date. She knew there was something about Nick's story that didn't add up, but her head was pounding and she decided she could dissect it later. Preferably after some sleep.

Looking up at him, she said, "Well, apparently I owe you a thank-you as well as an apology.

I wouldn't have picked you for the knight-in-shining-armor type, but in this case, I'm glad I was wrong."

She started to climb out, but Nick pressed his hand on her shoulder, stopping her. "We knight-in-armor types like to make sure our damsels get into the castle in one piece." He bent down to lift her out of the car, knowing she could easily walk the short distance to her door, but deciding to give in to his desire to hold her again. The hell with his knee.

Willa pushed against him, her pulse racing as her hands came into contact with his firm chest. "I'm okay. I can walk on my own." Seeing the determined look in his eyes, she continued more forcefully, "I know I fainted, but it was from drinking a little wine on an empty stom—ooomph."

Nick hoisted her over his shoulder, then turned back and hooked her purse with the handle of his cane. When she started to squirm, he lightly swatted her backside. "You sure don't play your damsel-in-distress part real well. Now stop wiggling or my surgeon will be able to pay for his yacht in one easy installment after I have to pay him to repair all the tendons you're ripping apart."

Willa stopped immediately, incensed at his

cavalier treatment of her, but not wanting to injure him.

"Thank you. Now, can you dig out your keys, please?" He swung her shoulder bag around where she could grab it.

"Let me guess, you played offense," she grumbled as she yanked the purse out of his hand. "I did faint, you know."

"All-pro for four straight years. And don't worry, this'll help get the blood circulating to the brain again." Having reached her door, he turned around, aiming her close to the knob. "Can you unlock it?"

"Put . . . me . . . down," she enunciated very slowly, her voice raspy—probably due in part to the proximity of her face to his firm tush. "Now."

Nick let her slide slowly down the front of his body, not trusting his knee enough to bend it to set her down. He was instantly aware that this method was proving hazardous to another part of his anatomy, one not so easily concealed in the tight jeans he was wearing.

As soon as her feet touched the ground, Nick stepped away from her. She felt relieved and curiously adrift all at the same time. "Sleep, I need sleep," she muttered.

Nick leaned down to ask her to repeat herself

at the same time as she turned to open the door. The action brought them face-to-face and, more disturbingly, mouth to mouth. Neither of them seemed capable of moving. He knew he was making a big mistake, but the throbbing in his knee as well as the one between his legs was making it impossible for him to think clearly.

Guided purely by instinct, he closed the gap between them. He traced her lips with small kisses, teasing her lips apart. She tasted exotic, a mixture of wine and something else that was all her own. He could get addicted to this.

As she softened against him he pulled her closer, leaning against the doorframe to take the weight off his knee so he could hold her with both arms. His lips just touching hers, he whispered, "Willa, open your eyes and look at me." She immediately complied, and Nick swallowed hard at the guarded desire he saw in her eyes. She wanted him, but she didn't want to. A nameless emotion welled up inside him, something very like regret, because she had every right to be wary of him. "We need to talk. You and I—"

"I know," Willa said softly, her voice so husky he could barely understand her. She kept her gaze locked with his for a moment, then pulled away, completely out of his arms.

He let her go, but not easily. Nick watched

her closely as she gathered her wits, struggling, but achieving a slightly ruffled version of her usual controlled self. It slowly occurred to him that her control was her defense, a shield she used to protect the passionate, more reckless side of her nature he'd glimpsed, and now tasted.

"Nick . . ."

He put his finger to her lips. "Don't say anything right now. It happened. I think we both know it had to happen." A slow smile curved his lips. "We'll talk about it tomorrow when I come over for breakfast." Her eyes narrowed danger-ously and he removed his finger from her lips.

"Wise move, considering how little I've eaten today," Willa said, her control ragged. "One little kiss and you think you can start giving orders." She ignored his sexy grin. "I have to go back in to work for a while tomorrow to catch up on some paperwork before the new training session starts. I really need every minute of sleep I can get. I know we need to talk"—she looked away for a moment, adding quietly—"about a lot of things." Looking back at him, she said, "But not now. Right now I'm going to bed. Alone."

Nick had the grace to look properly chastised at her pointed description of her actual Sunday-morning plans, but only for a moment. "Fine. You get some rest, and I'll be here at"—he looked at his watch, surprised that the glowing dial showed it was after midnight—"nine." She glared at him, so he added, "Thirty." *Still glaring.* "With breakfast." Before she strangled him, he clarified, "You need a ride to work, that is, unless you have a tractor or a horse around here. Besides, my recent elevation to knighthood brings with it a certain sense of responsibility."

When Willa remained silent, staring at him, he said in a dry tone, "I realize I should leave while most of my body parts are still intact, but I'm a glutton for punishment. Go on and say what's on your mind. We'll both sleep better."

After a long pause spent fighting the urge to smile back, Willa said simply, "Good night, Mr. Logan." She unlocked her door and stepped inside, surprised he hadn't stopped her. Just before she closed the door, she gave in to a wild impulse—a side of her that seemed to appear magically every time she got within a foot of him, and added, "I want to get into the office early. Be here at seven." She shut the door, then opened it again and said, "Thirty."

Nick threw his keys on the foyer table and picked up his portable phone as he limped down the short hallway to the kitchen. He punched in

Sky's number and pulled a cold beer from the fridge. Sky's groggy voice answered just as he propped his leg on the round pedestal table and pressed the cold beer against his knee.

"Uhh . . . hello?"

"Hey, Sky ol' buddy, not interrupting anything, am I?" Nick purposely kept his tone light, waiting for Sky to become fully alert before questioning him.

"At . . . two in the morning he's a comedian. Ol' buddy, my backside," Sky grumbled. He coughed and cleared his throat. "How'd the date go?"

Nick had never kept anything from Sky, but he wasn't exactly sure how to answer that one. "Let's just say Willa and Eric wouldn't get good ratings on *Love Connection*. Did you find anything?" When Willa's "date" with Eric had gone on and on, Nick had called Sky on his car phone and asked him to go over and check out Willa's office to see what, if anything, Eric had done while he was in there, and to lock up. Sky's next words confirmed Nick's suspicions.

"You were right, Nick. I don't know what they're up to, but I found several of those nice white packages stashed in Willa's office. Pretty well hidden too." Sky's voice was heavy with sarcasm and disappointment. "I guess she really is in this."

"No, Sky. She's not." Silence reigned for a moment as they both digested Nick's fervently spoken statement. He knew he'd been wavering in his belief about Willa's role in the mess, but until this moment he hadn't realized he'd made up his mind for good.

"What? Now you think she's innocent? What happened tonight, anyway?" Sky was clearly confused over his friend's abrupt about-face.

"Sky, I'd bet my Super Bowl rings that Eric is using her just like he used me. I don't know the whole story, but I'm going to see her in the morning and bring all of this out in the open. If I'm right, I'm going to ask her to help us."

"Boy, must have been some date," Sky murmured.

"Trust me on this one, okay, Sky?"

"I guess I don't have to add that *I* thought she was innocent from the start."

Nick cut into Sky's gloating statement. "What did you do with the packages?"

"The packages? Oh, I got rid of them."

"You what!"

"Calm down. I replaced them with powdered sugar. I called our man from the gym. He met me and picked them up."

"Powdered sugar, huh? I guess all those mystery books I brought in when you were in the hospital paid off." Nick hadn't forgotten the injury that had prematurely ended his friend's pro career—even if he was endlessly thankful that because of his misfortune, Sky had been available to help him out. "I'm still not too sure about Boxleitner."

"Nick, you've got to learn to trust the system eventually. Box swore he'd hold the stuff until we got some concrete evidence." Sky waited a beat, then added, "I still didn't tell him who we suspect, but I'm not so sure that now isn't the time to fill him in on the whole story."

Box was Frank Boxleitner, an old teammate of Sky's who was now with the DEA. Sky had kept in touch with him over the years and had convinced Nick that he would help him out. Nick had been skeptical, to say the least, his opinion of law enforcement in general not too high. When Box had ascertained that they didn't have any evidence directly implicating their suspect, he'd politely refrained from joining in the hunt, as his docket was full enough. But he had said that he would be more than glad to help once they had something concrete to go on.

"Maybe you're right. I guess I'm a little doubtful about people trusting my word of late.

After all, we're going to claim the most famous pro quarterback in the NFL is a coke addict who framed me to save his job—not exactly the most believable scenario. Just ask the Fairfax police." Nick twisted the beer open and took a long pull before asking, "Do you think the security monitors at the gym got Eric's activities on tape? If so, maybe we can bring Box in."

"I haven't watched the tapes yet, but based on where the stuff was stashed, he wouldn't necessarily have been in the line of the camera. He's a pretty sneaky bastard, Nick. I hope Willa knows what she's doing with him."

Nick had thought hard about the very same thing on the long drive home earlier that night. He realized now that that was when he'd decided to trust her—when his desire to protect her had outweighed his instinct to protect himself.

"Any prints on the bags?"

"Box said he'd check, but not to get our hopes up."

"Okay." Nick tried to keep the impatience out of his voice, but was only marginally successful. "Hey, thanks for helping out tonight. Couldn't do this without you, buddy."

"If it wasn't for you, I'd probably be in some mental ward reliving my pro days." Sky talked over Nick's attempt to shrug off the praise.

"Yeah, yeah, enough hearts and flowers. Get some sleep. In case you forgot, you've got a hot date early tomorrow morning with a beautiful redhead."

The incessant buzzing noise finally penetrated Willa's sleep. Without actually waking, she reached over and whacked the top of her clock radio to silence the annoying electronic alarm.

"It can't be morning," she groaned, and pulled a pillow over her head to block out the faint light that was filtering through her eyelids, proving her wrong. She knew she'd gone to sleep only a few minutes ago. Peering out from under her pillow, she slowly focused on the glowing blue numbers of her clock. *Six forty-five!*

In the next instant she shot up in bed, fully awake. Her mind was instantly alert and racing. *Nick will be here in less than an hour.* Willa threw back the bedspread and sheet and jumped out of bed—immediately grabbing onto the bedpost for support as her head swam. Her mind flashed instantly to the night before; memories of Nick's remedy for this affliction coming back in startling clarity.

As if the floodgates had been opened, the rest of the previous evening flowed through her mind, ending with Nick's breakfast bargain. *Me and my big mouth*, Willa berated herself silently, wishing she hadn't stubbornly insisted on an earlier time. She did have a lot of desk work to clear up—but it was her day off and she could get it done anytime. She headed toward the bathroom, stopping long enough to grab the silk kimono that doubled as her bathrobe from her oak armoire.

Emerging from her quick shower, she dropped the towel that had protected her hair from the steamy spray and put on the jade print robe. Her stomach loudly announced it was mealtime. Considering her lack of food yesterday and the wine she had for dinner, she was surprised she didn't have a headache this morning. But it couldn't hurt to arm herself with a mug of steaming coffee before facing Nick.

She opened the door leading out to the hallway and was instantly assailed by the delicious aroma of coffee. She wondered if all the fantasizing she'd been doing lately had raised her skills to new heights. No, she hadn't thought once of having any bacon. Either someone had broken into her house and decided to have a little breakfast before ripping her off, or . . . *Nick was there!*

She glanced back into her bedroom. Her clock read 7:15. The nerve of him, she thought, trying to intimidate her by arriving early! Furious at his pressure tactics, she stormed down the stairs, stomping hard on each plank, wishing it were Nick. Her bare feet didn't make nearly enough noise, and that made her even angrier.

She pushed through the swinging doors that led into the kitchen and came to a halt, hands curled into fists on her hips. "Who gave you permission to come into my home? When I told you seven-thirty, I meant it." She didn't want to notice how incredibly male he looked. His well-worn jeans pulled tightly across his thighs and the sleeves of his faded blue-and-white T-shirt tugged into snug bands above his well-developed biceps.

It took several seconds before she noticed the design emblazoned across his shirt. The Jaguars' logo. Well, she thought, her steam building to the boiling point, if he was trying to add to her guilt by advertising the team he'd been banned from . . . it was working. Dammit.

Nick took the opportunity her slight pause gave him. "Good morning, Princess." Her eyes narrowed at the pet name, but he didn't mind. She stood there with her hair all wild and fiery, like her temperament. Her stance caused the front of her satiny green robe to gape open slightly, revealing the soft inner curves of her breasts. She was nothing short of magnificent.

At that moment she could have said anything and he wouldn't have cared. Because he knew, then and there, that they were destined to be lovers. They had to be.

Willa swore she could feel his electric-blue gaze consume her. It made her skin sizzle—the sensation dancing across her body like water droplets skittering over a hot griddle. Following his gaze downward, she realized why. Blushing, furious at the rapidly increasing rate he managed to make her do so, she resisted the urge to fold her arms in front of her. *Two could play at this game.* She purposely let her gaze travel slowly over his body.

It took only a few seconds to realize that her ploy was backfiring. Her skin hadn't cooled a bit—in fact, she was certain her entire body had a rosy glow. A glance at Nick's sparkling eyes told her he was aware of her faulty strategy, but he didn't seem to mind at all. Judging from his grin, he was loving every minute of it.

"I did knock," he said finally, his tone matching his sexy grin. "But you didn't answer. You know, even way out here, you should be more careful about locking your doors." He turned back to the stove to tend to whatever was hissing and crackling.

Over his shoulder he added, his voice the epitome of nonchalance, "As much as I love that robe, if we're going to get any talking done, you'd better go put some more clothes on."

Silence. He turned back around.

She looked as though she was debating the merits of various methods of murder. Nick decided his best defense was a good offense. His specialty. He let his gaze rest on the enticing area of skin exposed by the parted robe. Smiling wickedly, he tapped the spatula he was holding against his chin as if trying to grasp an elusive thought. His eyes lit up as he hit on it. "I've got it. Jasmine, right? Great scent." He turned back to the stove as her mouth dropped open, and calmly said, "Now hurry, breakfast is almost ready."

FIVE

Willa opened her mouth then snapped it shut, deciding it would be best if she left the room, not caring what he read into her compliance with his arrogant request. The country kitchen she'd always wished was smaller and cozier had suddenly become far too intimate.

She dressed quickly, reassuring herself that the only reason she hadn't told Nick to take a hike was because her stomach never would have forgiven her. She immediately recalled exactly what she'd hungered for a few moments ago. *Damn his sexy hide*, she swore silently, disgusted at her lack of control around him. The picture of sweet charm one minute, then arrogant self-confidence the next. And the total package appealed to her more than she cared to admit. She needed to slow down and figure things out before she went crazy.

"Breakfast is ready."

Nick's announcement boomed up the stairway, startling Willa. The time had come to tell him her side of it. Her weak plan to draw a confession out of Eric would never work. Had she really thought she could use her feminine wiles to get him to talk? She'd never quite figured what those wiles were, anyway . . . as Eric had pointed out. She gave a humorless laugh. Playing ball wasn't the only thing Nick and Eric did well—and when it came to womanly charms, she was definitely in the rank-amateur league.

Her eyes lit up as she had a sudden idea. She dashed back into her room and dug through the explosion of clothes crammed into her armoire. "Aha!" She pulled on her favorite shirt like a battle shield and smiled at her reflection in the mirror. If she was going to have to play with the big boys, at least she'd have a team shirt on.

Nick went through the motions of preparing breakfast, his mind still dwelling on Willa in that Oriental robe. It was only the second time he'd seen her in anything other than sweats—and he couldn't believe the restraint it had taken not to cross the room and convince her to let him touch that creamy skin so erotically wrapped in silk, to taste it.

Hearing hinges squeak, Nick turned and all thoughts of jade silk and frying bacon took flight. For erotic attire, nothing beat faded black jeans molded to legs that went on forever. So it was understandable that it took a second or two for him to notice the familiar red-and-white shirt she was wearing.

The last time he'd seen that emblem, the bulges under it had been formed by heavy padding. "The Carolina Rebels!" he shouted. Hostile feelings about his former team's nemesis were ingrained and hadn't disappeared simply because he no longer played the game.

"My favorite team," Willa answered honestly, pointedly looking at Nick's shirt.

Nick grimaced. His innocent choice of apparel must have come off looking like a direct challenge. "How could you be a Rebels fan? Your dad played for the Jaguars."

"When Dad was first drafted into the NFL, he played for Carolina." Nick nodded, familiar with her father's career. "Well, the Rebels were a new team at the time and not very good." He smiled in agreement. "I always liked to root for the underdog, and when Dad was traded to the Jaguars a few years later, I was already a diehard fan."

"He wasn't upset when you rooted for the enemy?"

"Heavens no. He encouraged me to maintain my loyalties. Besides," she added, smiling broadly as she reminisced, "it was something to argue about. Dad loved a good debate."

"I have a feeling that's an inherited trait."

Willa looked at Nick, her eyes shining in agreement before her smile turned wistful. "I haven't thought about those days, before I went to college . . ." *Before Dad got sick*, she thought, looking beyond Nick, into her past.

"I thought your dad was a great man. At least as far as football was concerned," Nick commented quietly. The pain that shadowed her eyes for a moment bothered him. He felt bad that what had started as a warm memory for her had somehow turned sad. "You loved him very much." She didn't have to answer for Nick to see the depth of feeling she had for her deceased father. It shone in her face and in her eyes. For a blazing instant Nick knew a deep-seated need, stronger than anything he'd ever felt, to be the recipient of that kind of look. From her.

A little taken aback by the ferocious wave of desire that engulfed him, Nick frowned and turned back to the counter. In a tone sharper than he intended, he said, "Set the table if you plan on eating this while it's still warm."

Her smile evaporated at his change and sharp words. *Had she imagined the scene that had just taken place?* It seemed like every time they made a connection of some kind, something happened to break it. But for the life of her, this time she couldn't guess what it was. She was curious about the almost desperate look that had briefly registered on Nick's face when he commented on her love for her dad. *Maybe I imagined that too.*

Frustrated that she couldn't be around Nick for ten minutes without losing her temper, she determined to be civil, no matter his mood. "The plates are in the upper left cabinet. I'll pour the coffee and get the silver."

Nick seemed to accept her unspoken request for a truce. He waited until they were seated and eating before he spoke. "I'm sorry I snapped."

Willa looked up from her plate and saw that he was sincere. She shrugged, but didn't chance talking quite yet.

"If you want to talk about him, I don't mind. It might help me understand so I don't inadvertently hurt you in the future."

A part of her locked onto the word "future." "We, that is my dad and I, moved around a lot as he moved around the league. We settled in Virginia just as I started high school and I finally thought I'd found my niche."

"And did you?"

A smile wandered across her face. "No. I grew six inches before my junior year. The only boys taller than me were the guys on the basketball team, and their interest in me was limited to getting me to play b-ball and getting Jaguar's autographs. When it came to anything social, they chose the petite cheerleader types."

"They must have been blind," Nick muttered. Willa glanced up at him and he nodded for her to go on.

"Being tall and gawky was bad enough, but people always seemed to expect me to be something special because I had a famous dad, which made me feel doubly awkward. I constantly failed to measure up to everyone's expectations. So I concentrated on studying instead. Then, when I was a senior, I discovered my long legs were actually good for something."

Unbidden images of her long legs wrapped around his waist wreaked havoc with Nick's senses and he forced his gaze to the untouched food on his plate, certain that the use she had discovered for her legs couldn't come close to the one he'd imagined.

". . . track and field," she finished, then

glanced up when Nick let out an audible sigh of relief. "Anyway, the point is, I spent most of my school years—high school and later college—on the track, or buried in a textbook. My dream was to open my own pro training facility one day. Still is."

"You said you and your dad. What about your mom?"

"My mom died when I was very young." She put her fork back on her plate. "I don't remember her at all." Her voice softened as she spoke. "Dad used to tell me how much that would have bothered her, since she was the one who got up a dozen times a night with me when I was a baby."

"A real tyrant right from the start, huh?" Nick chuckled, hoping this time he could sustain the rapport developing between them for more than a few minutes.

"My mom used to pretend not to hear me until my dad got so fed up with my caterwauling that he'd get up. It was his favorite 'poor dad' story, but I don't think he really minded."

A picture of a tiny baby with soft red curls came unbidden into Nick's mind. "I don't think I'd mind either." He didn't realize he had spoken out loud until Willa cleared her throat. To cover his embarrassment he asked, "You ever think about having kids?"

"Sure. I didn't have any close relatives, my parents were only children, and I used to fantasize about having dozens of brothers and sisters to play with." Her face was dreamy, but also shadowed with pain.

She quickly concealed it, but not before Nick, who'd forgotten his food the moment she started speaking, noticed. "Why didn't your dad remarry? Would it have bothered you?"

"No, I don't remember my mom. I would have welcomed the chance to have one. But Dad said he'd already found the love of his life and he was content with that." Willa had never truly understood that, not believing that in a whole world filled with people, there could be only one perfect mate for each person. She shivered involuntarily when she looked up to find Nick intently staring at her. She realized, somewhat uncomfortably, that her dad's feelings were becoming easier to understand all the time. "Do you have any brothers and sisters?" she asked a bit too brightly.

"Nope, just me. Dad said I was enough of a handful and he wouldn't subject his worst enemy, much less my mother, to dealing with two of me."

"They sound like smart people," she teased, unable to resist. "Do you see them often?"

"They're both dead." When she looked

guilty for asking such a potentially painful question, Nick quickly reassured her. "It's okay. It was sad, but not tragic. My parents were older when they had me. Dad had a bad heart and died a number of years ago. Mom died shortly after."

Nick stopped for a moment, then said, "She died in her sleep, but I always kind of thought she just wanted to be with Dad." He felt uncomfortable, and a little shocked, that he'd revealed thoughts he'd never shared with anyone—not even Sky—and his voice turned brusque. "I'm damned glad they weren't around to see me arrested."

As soon as the words were out of his mouth, he realized who he was saying them to. Both of them were startled into silence by the abrupt return to reality. Nick and Willa looked at each other for a long moment, neither knowing what to say to defuse the suddenly charged atmosphere.

Willa escaped by rising and carrying her empty plate to the sink. She hadn't even remembered eating during her conversation with Nick. Was the warm intimacy they had shared just an illusion?

She braced her hands on the sink, drawing in her breath and her courage before turning to face him. He was standing right behind her and she came smack up against the hard wall of his chest. She stared at the word "Jaguars" for a long time before finding the nerve to look up at him. Her eyes widened in surprise. The hostility and accusation she'd expected to find weren't there.

"Willa, I know we have a lot to discuss," he said seriously. A hint of that knee-weakening smile surfaced as he added, "I guess that would take the prize for the understatement of the year." At her pained attempt at returning his smile, he said more soothingly, "I honestly don't understand what role you played in all of this, but I can't ignore that something else is happening here."

Willa's eyes misted slightly, and her lower lip trembled, knowing that that "something else" would end this morning before it really had a chance to begin. "I, uh . . ." She cleared her throat, trying in vain to dislodge the sudden lump there. "Nick, before I explain, I want you to know that I never meant to hurt you."

Nick's eyes narrowed at her choice of words, and Willa knew she'd been right when she saw the warmth in his blue irises slowly fade to an icy shade of steel. Chilled to the core, she said, "I know you believe I helped ruin your career, but give me a chance to explain."

Nick's brain shouted at him to come to his

senses; after all, she had just admitted her guilt. What more did he need to know to end his silly infatuation? And he knew then that he was doomed, because when he looked into those green eyes glittering with tears, guilt showing as plainly as if she had spoken the words, God help him, all he wanted to do was take her in his arms and kiss her until he could shake the crazy idea that, like their parents, he, too, had found his one and only.

Unable to stop the thought from becoming the deed, he pulled her tightly against him, molding her body to his, exulting in the perfect fit. His kiss was both seeking and punishing; trying to find the answers to his questions while chastising her for making him feel so strongly.

Willa responded immediately. Whatever else happened, they shared something unique that neither had the strength to deny. Even as her words had extinguished the light in his eyes, she knew the flame of desire burned too hot to stop him from kissing her—or her from responding. It was as if, by kissing her, he could use her response to him as punishment for her guilt.

It soon became obvious to them both that if this was a form of punishment, they were sharing the same jail cell.

Nick pulled away first, tilting his head back

slightly to suck in a lungful of air. He rubbed his hand over his face, his other arm kept her molded to his body, his hips kept her pressed against the counter.

She didn't try to pull away, not because she thought he wouldn't let her, but because she didn't want it to be over so soon. Given the close proximity of their bodies, Nick's response to their kiss was very evident. She braved a look at his stormy eyes. The confusion she saw was both encouraging and disheartening.

"Nick, I want—no, I need—to tell you what happened last summer." He started to say something, but she placed a finger on his lips; the texture and warmth of his soft flesh almost undid her resolve. "You have to hear me out. It's the only way I'm going to get through it."

Nick seemed to consider her statement, then released her. Turning back toward the table, he picked up his coffee mug and without a word pushed through the kitchen door.

Willa grabbed the counter behind her for support. How could he be so passionate one minute and so remote the next? Could it be possible the kiss hadn't affected him too?

She drew on every ounce of strength she possessed to collect her scattered emotions and form them into some semblance of resolve. Collecting her coffee mug, she pushed through the swinging door after him, determined to keep him there until he heard her side of the story. What happened after that she would have to leave to fate.

Willa found Nick staring out of the huge window in the living room. It was her favorite room, the cozy, worn furnishings attesting to the fact that the room was used frequently. Willa loved the view of her small patch of unspoiled Virginia countryside and was secretly glad Nick had chosen this room for their confrontation. And she was certain that confrontation adequately described what was about to take place.

"Nick, I need you to listen. Really listen." She waited for him to turn, knowing that no matter how difficult it proved to be, she had to look at him while she spoke.

If his shuttered eyes hadn't destroyed her confidence, his words killed her hopes completely. "Just tell me straight out. Spare me any theatrics or emotional requests for my support. I want the whole story. Don't leave anything out." He watched her facade of control crumble, and added a bit more gently, "This is my life, Willa. Please, tell me the truth."

She wanted to go to him, to hold him and soothe his wounded pride, to try to renew his faith in her innocence. But that was exactly what he'd asked her not to do. So she took a deep breath and began.

"First, you have to understand what my life was like before I met Eric." The scowl that engulfed Nick's face at the mention of Eric's name wasn't encouraging.

"I gather from what you've already told me that you were more or less ripe for the picking," he said bluntly.

Willa winced at his painful but accurate assessment. "When Eric showed interest in me, I was more than just flattered. I was shocked. By the time he joined the team and went on to become a star, I was in college, so I'd never met him." *Or you,* she thought, then dismissed that line of thinking; it would only make her more nervous. Willa took a fortifying sip of coffee before going on. "My father had passed away several years before and I was in school getting my master's, so my contact with the team was limited to an occasional visit to Doc Abbott. Actually I met Eric while visiting Doc at the practice field." Willa glanced down into her mug barely noticing Nick's increased attention at the mention of her old friend.

"Is that where you always met Doc?"

Startled by the question, she looked up at Nick, but his expression was still closed. "It depended on the time of the year. If it was during football season, I'd drop by the team's practice facility. If not, I went to his office in Alexandria. Why?"

"Just curious. Go on." Nick wasn't encouraged. This meant she had easy access to the team's facilities.

"As I said, when Eric asked me out, I was surprised."

"With your looks and athletic figure, I'm sure men weren't shy around you."

Willa shrugged off the compliments, a bit disappointed that Nick still didn't seem to understand—or want to. "By the time I got to college, I was so immersed in my studies, and in sports, that I didn't have much time for romance." When Nick snorted in disbelief, Willa responded immediately, her tone definitely defensive. "Any spare time I had at the beginning of school was spent with my dad. His death was the result of a long, ugly battle with cancer. I had more important things to worry about than whether or not I had a date Friday night."

"I'm sorry about your dad and what you must have gone through," Nick said in response to her emotional outburst. "I don't mean to sound unfeeling, but I still find it hard to believe that your father's illness kept men from seeking you out and at least asking for a date."

"Well, as you've probably surmised, I can be a bit defensive at times."

"A bit," he responded dryly.

Willa wasn't sure if she should be offended by the remark or relieved that he still had his sense of humor. "During my father's illness I guess I became overly sensitive to intrusions on our private lives. Dad had always handled the media, but when he became ill, that job fell to me." She clenched her hands tightly around the mug as she replayed the memories of that difficult time in her life.

"The press hounded him all the time, trying to exploit his pain for the sake of what they termed a 'human-interest story.' I didn't see it that way. One result was that I wasn't the most approachable female in the world."

"Which brings us back to Eric," Nick said. "I assume he was persistent enough to approach the unapproachable. His ego is certainly big enough."

Surprising Nick, Willa agreed. "It certainly was. I mistook his bulging ego for confidence, and was overwhelmed by it. No one had ever pursued me like that."

"Didn't that make you the least bit suspicious?" Nick wanted to bite his tongue at the obvious pain his question inflicted on her already bruised pride, but he had to know.

"It sounds hard to believe now, but I never really gave it much thought. Eric can be very convincing. And I have to admit that a part of me felt avenged."

"Avenged? How?"

"I guess I got carried away with the idea that someone as famous as Eric could have the hots for Willow-tree Trask."

It was said so ingenuously that Nick didn't doubt for a second that it was the truth. She wasn't the hard, calculating ice princess he'd thought—hoped?—she'd be.

He walked over and sat down beside her, cursing silently when she pulled away. "Can you tell me more about Doc?"

Willa stiffened, then forcibly relaxed, but kept from touching him. "What exactly do you want to know?"

"Well, if Eric couldn't test clean because of his drug habit, then he'd need an inside track to either the head coach or the team doctor in order to switch the test results. I figure it's Doc and he used you to get to him somehow."

Before she could answer, he fired another question at her.

"Why, after eight months, did you suddenly

think Eric had been up to something? And why did it take you so long to remember me?" Nick knew this was difficult for her and wanted nothing more than to pull her into his arms, but they needed to get this over with first.

"I, uh . . . overheard you and Sky the night we met." Willa hurried on before she lost her nerve. "I don't make a habit of listening in on conversations, but I heard my name and—"

"You only found out two days ago?" Willa looked at him then. Her face was flaming in embarrassment, and he knew she spoke the truth. It certainly explained a lot, and it went a long way toward easing any lingering doubts about her innocence.

"It was one of the biggest shocks of my life," Willa said into the silence. "Things were crazy then. I was going through a lot, juggling school and my relationship with Eric. I didn't keep up with the news, and after I broke off with Eric—I especially avoided football. I heard about the arrest and the trial, but I'd never met you and I didn't give it much thought. Nick, I didn't know." Willa turned her face away, squeezing back the threat of tears, achingly aware that her blind trust and stupidity had cost him his career. "Those packages—the ones I took to Eric—I really thought they were vitamins," she said, her voice quiet, "but I guess they must have been cocaine."

"What were you doing with them anyway?"

"You know athletes consume large amounts of supplements to meet the extra demands they place on their bodies."

"So why didn't he just have his dealer deliver his 'vitamins' to him personally? Why involve you?"

"He told me it was more convenient. You know the Jaguars' practice is closed to the public. But because of my dad and my friendship with Doc, I can come and go as I please. So it was easier for me to drop them off." Her heart filled her throat as the full impact of her role in his downfall hit her. "God, I never thought twice about it."

Nick gave in to the need to touch her and gently tugged at her shoulders until she'd turned back to him. He wanted to kiss the tears tipping her lashes, but doggedly continued his questioning, knowing it was best for both of them to get it all out in the open now. "Who did you leave the stuff with?"

Willa struggled to get a grip on herself, needing to finish without falling completely apart. "I'd usually pop in to see Doc and he'd hold them for Eric until after practice."

Nick remained silent, and Willa was unsure of the direction of his thoughts. When he finally spoke, his voice was deep, and carried a trace of pain.

"Why didn't you tell me all this that first night?"

"Because I knew you had every reason not to trust me. You didn't exactly sound reasonable on the subject of my involvement, so I decided to get proof. That's why I agreed to see Eric when he called that night."

"You only went out with him to get information?" Willa nodded and Nick sighed and pulled her into his arms, holding her long and hard before he could go on. Knowing now the shock she must have suffered, he was amazed and impressed that she was able to get it together enough to handle it as she had. His heart made another giant leap in her direction. He lifted her chin, needing to look into her so-expressive eyes when he asked her. "I pretty much know how they did it, but I still want to know why they used me. I just need proof." His clear blue eyes drilled into hers with an intensity she'd never seen. "Will you help me prove that Eric and Doc set me up?"

Willa hadn't been aware she was holding her breath until it came out in a whoosh at his sincerely spoken request. But the beginnings of hope were tempered by his accusation against Doc. Carefully choosing her words, she said, "I want to help you, Nick, but I refuse to implicate Doc. He's like a second father to me. He would never willingly be involved in this, or involve me. I'm sure of that."

Nick was silent for a moment and Willa braced herself for another argument. She was confused and tired. She really wanted to help Nick, but on this issue she would not back down. When the lengthening silence became intolerable, she asked, "Do you really want to chance working with me?"

Nick didn't miss the vulnerable tone in her voice. "I believe you, Willa. I want your help, if you're willing to give it."

"Absolutely. It's just that we obviously don't agree on everything." Nick raised an eyebrow, a dry smile quirking the corners of his mouth. Willa felt like she'd been given a precious gift at the return of the warmth in his eyes. Allowing a small smile herself, she added, "Well, you have to admit, every time we're together for more than ten minutes, we either end up arguing or kiss . . . ing." The last part of her sentence came out on a gulp. The flash of desire in Nick's eyes was instant and consumed her with heat.

His smile broadened into a sexy grin, his eyes

flashed a deeper blue. "I'm willing to run the risk if you are."

Willa could only smile in return. It seemed as if all her bodily fluids were pooling in her lap, rendering her mouth dry and her lips incapable of forming words. Which was just as well. When he looked at her like that, her mind conjured up all sorts of impulsive and unwise ideas.

Torn between wanting to respond to the sparkle of desire in her emerald-green eyes and the vulnerability he sensed lay just beneath, Nick wondered what she'd say if he told her he'd be content to spend the rest of the day making slow, sweet love to her right here on the couch. Chivalry finally won out. Sometimes being a knight was just no fun.

Nick satisfied himself with one gentle kiss, which he placed between her eyebrows; anything more would be too risky. "Why don't we let the subject rest for a while? If you don't have to be in to work right away, maybe you can give me a tour of the place. That barn out back looks straight out of a jigsaw-puzzle picture."

Willa fought the urge to lift her face to his when he bent to brush a soft kiss on her forehead. She knew he was right, they needed a break from their problems—and some time to sort out what exactly was happening between them.

"What do you say?"

His smile was angelic, but the gleam in his eyes was devilish. Willa's sense of self-preservation took over and she scrambled out of his arms. "Come on, I'll race you to the back door."

"You'd race a cripple? Heartless woman!"

SIX

Nick walked through the lofty barn. The stalls had been torn out; the hayloft ran across the top of a third of the otherwise cavernous space. He reached up and, even as tall as he was, was barely able to pull out a weathered piece of old straw peeking between the slatted boards.

Twirling it, he continued to investigate, determined to keep his mind off kissing Willa.

"This is incredible. You say your dad never used it?"

Even the innocent piece of straw between his fingers evoked provocative thoughts. His mind drifted to haylofts, which led directly to visions of lovemaking and Willa's red hair spread like wildfire over the yellow straw, her long legs wrapped around his hips—

"Dad never used this barn like he wanted to.

He became ill while renovating this place. He wanted to get into racing cars." She gestured to an oblong structure covered with tarp, barely discernible in the shadows at the opposite end of the building. "That's the extent of his collection there."

"Can I look?" Willa nodded and Nick made his way to the covered automobile. Expecting to see a carefully preserved hot rod, he let out a surprised laugh when he uncovered a rusting Corvair. "This is your father's idea of a race car?"

Willa smiled at his mocking laugh, forcing her thoughts away from how large and powerful he looked. Even in the drafty old cavern of a barn, he dominated the space. "His dream was to race in those cross-country rallies held by old-car enthusiasts. But I think he mostly wanted a chance to renovate the cars." Her smile turned a bit wistful as she dragged the tarp back over the Corvair.

He'd refrained from touching her the entire hour they'd prowled around the grounds. He'd naively thought being in a creaking old barn would keep his thoughts on the straight and narrow, allowing him just to get to know her without all the swirling emotional stuff. But it was hard to separate the conscious idea of learning everything about this complex lady from the powerful subconscious emotional tugs he had no control over—not to mention the physical ache of being near her and wanting to hold her, touch her. Why did he have to pick now to fall in—

Whoa, Jack. Had he actually considered even *thinking* about the L-word?

No. No way. So she intrigued the hell out of him, even with her prickly thorns designed to keep him from discovering the petal-soft core of the woman he believed her to be. He didn't blame her for being defensive. Hell, everyone she'd ever loved had either died on her or abused her love and trust. So what if *he* trusted her? Big deal. And he'd never consciously hurt her. And, dammit, yes, he'd like to wring the neck of anyone who had. It didn't really mean he loved her.

"Nick? What's wrong? It's your knee, isn't it?" Willa frowned as she came over to him. "I told you we shouldn't walk so much."

"You're sore 'cause I beat you to the back door," he answered, trying to grin and hoping she'd let it go.

"Nick, I'm serious. Maybe we'd better head back."

He tried to keep up his teasing front but couldn't. He imagined how wonderful it would be to accept the honest concern he read in her emerald-green eyes. It had been so long since anyone had really given a damn about him, he didn't quite know how to handle the things she made him feel. She stood in front of him, concern etched into every feature, with more of that damned straw sticking out of her wild red hair. All legs and arms, curls and straw, she should have resembled nothing more than a gawky scarecrow. Yet he'd never been so completely aroused by anyone in his entire life. He wanted nothing more than to scoop her into his arms, carry her up to the loft, and spread that flame of hair over a bed of hay while pushing slowly into her warmth. . . .

Groaning, he hung his head, rubbed a hand over his face, and gave up the fight. Unable to look up, he simply reached out his hand. After what seemed like an eternity, he felt her strong, slender fingers slide between his. Sighing deeply, he leaned against the tarp-covered car and pulled her between his thighs, his lips landing on hers like a perfectly executed pass, his finesse born of a natural talent that only she seemed able to inspire.

Running his free hand up along her hip, he dropped her arm around his waist, then continued higher to delve his fingers beneath the tumble of curls flowing around her shoulders. "Willa, I need—"

"I know, Nick." Her voice was wine deep.

"I tried not to, but—"

"Shhhh . . . our ten minutes are up." Willa gave herself to him freely. The dull ache she felt whenever she thought of her father and the dreams he'd left unfulfilled dimmed in comparison with the pain she felt as she'd watched the look of desire and longing in Nick's face a moment ago turn slowly into a fierce scowl. That pain was intensified by the knowledge that he didn't want to want her—and she still didn't care. She knew how incredibly foolish it was even to think about anything resembling a future with this man—but God help her, she knew it was too late not to be devastated when he left. And she wanted what little bit fate saw fit to grant her and to hell with the aftermath. At least this time she knew what to expect.

With that one thought in mind, she gave herself up to the passion that had sparked between them.

Nick's lips left hers and traveled across her cheek, stopping to nibble at the soft pink lobe and the soft skin underneath. "I'm sorry about your dad, Willa," he said softly, his voice hoarse even as he made a last, desperate attempt to retain a hold on coherent thought.

He wanted to tell her he understood her pain,

and how hard it was for her to trust. That he wouldn't hurt her. That she could trust him. But in that instant she moved against him, pressing the full length of her body to his. "Good Lord, Willa, you're turning me inside out." He pulled her hand up to his chest and captured it between their bodies, then molded her hips to his, feeling an immediate all-consuming need to share with her the fiery heat that consumed him with a mere touch, a soft kiss.

Willa clenched a handful of his shirt, unable to prevent an answering moan to the hard ridge of desire that was pressed against her belly. She raised her face to his, reveling in the tempest she saw raging in his stormy eyes. "I'm sorry, too, Nick." Her voice was all brandy and heat. "So sorry for everything."

Nick pulled her back against his chest. "I know, baby. I know. Me too." A tiny thread of rational thought pulled at his inner core with her fervently spoken apology. He fought to diminish his overwhelming need, more than a little afraid he'd be unequal to the task.

He freely admitted that what was happening between them scared the living daylights out of him. The instincts he'd relied on all of his life, the ones he'd honed to perfection over the last eight months, had gone completely haywire. The woman he'd only days ago been convinced had destroyed everything he'd held dear was fast becoming the only thing worth giving a damn about.

"Willa?" He felt her nod against his chest, her breathing still fast and hard. "I trust you. And, Lord knows, I want you. But I think we need to slow down a bit. This is . . ." He'd been about to say insanity, but instead finished with, "It's happening too fast. Do you understand?"

Willa's mind raced along with her pulse. She had been swept into another realm by his fierce kisses and gentle caresses. She heard what he was saying, and a part of her understood intimately the wisdom of his words. But deep inside, the very center of her being had gravitated to something new and sparkling. That tantalizing peek of what lay in store between them tempted her to try anything, everything, she could think of to see it through to the end. But her history of hurt and betrayal, along with her present situation, ultimately governed her head, if not her heart.

"Yes, I understand." Stifling the small instinctive cry when she moved out of his arms, leaving his touch, she wandered toward the shaft of sunlight streaming through the double doors. "Would you like to see the rest of the place?"

Nick stood there, feeling bereft and strangely halved, like holding her made him somehow complete. Kicking himself for stopping, he also knew he'd done the right thing. Until this whole mess was sorted out, he had to keep some sense of self—which meant not kissing, touching, or holding Willa. He watched her turn back to him, waiting for his answer, and he sent a silent warning to all five feet ten inches of wild red hair, full breasts, and legs that went on forever.

Look out, Princess, because after we nail Miller and the not-so-good Dr. Abbott, I'm coming after you. And I intend to touch, kiss, and hold you as much as I want for the rest of our lives.

The decision made, he found it easier to smile as he nodded and followed her out into the bright spring sunshine.

Willa led them back to the house an hour later. Nick had insisted on tramping over the entire ten acres. Even with a cane, she marveled at his natural agility as he moved easily over the uneven ground. His energy seemed endless, but eventually it became impossible for him to hide the growing stiffness in his knee from her trained eye. Even then, only threats of a severely torturous rehab session, devised solely by her, got him to agree to go in.

"Go on to the front room and prop up your knee. I'll fix us some iced tea."

Nick nodded, not pausing as he hobbled

down the hallway, glad she would be kept busy in the kitchen for a few minutes while he checked to see if he'd been hallucinat— "Damn!" he swore as he reached the large picture window, barely catching a flash of black at the curve in the driveway through the cloud of slowly settling dust. Eric's Porsche. He'd bet money on it. He cursed himself for staying out for so long because of the uncontrollable hormone surge he experienced whenever she so much as laughed. Because of his lack of control over himself, he'd just missed catching that filthy bastard Eric red-handed.

He'd discussed with Sky the probable reasons Eric had for stashing the drugs in Willa's office. They figured it was to ensure her compliance with whatever new scheme he'd dreamed up. They'd also agreed—actually Nick had convinced Sky—not to tell Willa about it. She was nervous enough, and knowing how desperate Miller had become might make her too nervous to convince him to talk. But Nick had misjudged Eric again. He never thought he'd go this far.

His hatred of his former teammate increased to an almost blinding red haze. Nick played a rough sport and played to win, but he was not the kind of guy who solved things off the field by bashing heads. Right now, though, he wanted to bash more than Eric's *head*. Because the bastard had involved Willa, put her directly in danger, Nick wanted to twist Eric's conniving little neck.

Nick prowled the room, poking at possible hiding places and trying to burn off some steam. The urge to kill another person was startling to contend with. But the realization that he'd come to feel this strongly only after Willa had been threatened shook him to the core.

He heard her footsteps and reluctantly moved to the old overstuffed sofa. He'd have to find a way to search her house more thoroughly, but as it was, he barely got his leg extended along the plump cushions before she entered the room carrying two tall glasses of iced tea.

"So what did you think?"

Momentarily nonplussed, he asked, "About what?"

"The farm. The way you covered every square inch, I thought you were going to make me an offer on the place."

The smile on her face was more relaxed than he'd seen it, and, for the present, worry free. He vowed to keep it that way as long as he could and subdued his concern for her safety, for now. Recalling her question, he smiled and responded honestly. "Actually I thought it would be a great place for my kids."

Willa blanched. Oh my Lord! Never in all

the moments she had dreamed, fantasized, and in general just lusted over him had she given any thought to whether he was married . . . or maybe he was divorced. No, she thought morosely, with her track record he'd probably been married since high school and had four kids. She reminded herself that she trusted him, that while he needed her to help him, surely he wouldn't do that to her. Still, her voice, when she spoke, was a bit squeaky. "*Your* kids?"

The myriad of expressions that flitted across her face in those few seconds were touching in the depth of vulnerability they revealed, but they were also comically priceless. Nick fought it, but lost the battle and laughed out loud. He laughed so hard that he lost his balance, prompting Willa instinctively to leap out of her chair and brace a steadying hand on his hip. His laughter died the instant she touched him and the resulting flame of desire shot through his body. Only the honest concern on her face kept the light twinkling in his blue eyes.

"What is so funny about my wanting to know if you have children?" she demanded, increasing the pressure on her hand until they were almost nose to nose.

"Just don't ever play poker, Princess."

"Huh? Poker? And what's with all this princess stuff." She knew she was overreacting, but a lifetime spent being the source of jokes, along with her damned reaction to being this close to him, loving the purely male scent of him even as he laughed at her, made her angry.

"I'm sorry I laughed, but I wasn't being cruel, honest." When she would have moved away, he placed his palm on her cheek, caressing her clenched jaw until her mutinous expression softened. He turned serious, his smile gentle. "When I first found out about you and Eric, I was, understandably, a little upset. I had you all figured out as this devious, manipulative gold digger. Sky told me I was wrong, but being a hardheaded jock, I had to find out for myself. Then, last night, when you fainted and I brought you home . . . I don't know, Willa, I guess you made me feel needed." He reached up to tuck a wayward curl behind her ear. "Until that moment I didn't realize how much I needed that. You were my damsel in distress. The princess in need of a knight." Embarrassed now, he focused his gaze on her mouth. "I don't know, maybe it's silly, but in a lot of ways"—he looked back up at her—"the image fits you."

As before, Willa wore her emotions in her eyes, and when they became a bit glassy, Nick bit down hard on his inner cheek, forcing a light tone into a conversation that was heading back into dangerous waters. "As for the kids, they're not mine exact—"

"You meant your camp kids, didn't you?" Willa didn't need for him to answer. "I'm such a jerk."

Nick guided her hand, the one still gripping her iced tea, to his lips and took a sip. "No, you're not. You're just gun-shy." He held her gaze, his smile fading. "At least you asked me instead of just assuming you were right. Your trust means a lot to me, Willa." He broke their gaze and swung his leg gently to the floor and helped Willa from her awkward position until they were both standing up. "I should get you in to work and retrieve your wheels." Forcing his hands to release her, he shifted away from her.

"Right. Let me get my purse." Reluctantly, but with something that felt shamefully like relief, Willa accepted his suggestion. As it was, he'd tugged at so many of her heartstrings she felt like a marionette. As soon as he'd left the house, she raced upstairs for her gym bag, as if she could outrun the pain that had squeezed her heart at the blatant look of failure in his eyes when he'd spoken of his kids. They'd regarded him as a hero—and she'd been partly to blame for killing the dream for Nick and the kids he helped. He'd never forgive her for that. And she wouldn't blame him.

Willa intentionally kept the conversation light on their drive back to the shopping district of Tyson's Corner, steering the subject to safe ground every time Nick tried to get serious. She knew her bubble would have to burst, but couldn't help wanting to preserve the fragile feeling for as long as she could. The morning spent with Nick had been, even with all the emotional upheaval, one of the best in her life.

As he pulled the large sedan into Devon's parking lot, she turned to look at Nick, his blue eyes deepening to that sensual stormy shade as their gazes locked and held. Sensing her bubble had just hit the breaking point, she broke away first and began digging in her purse. "I know I put them in here somewh—"

"Willa." Nick put his hand on her arm. "I know this morning—hell, the whole past couple of days—have been pretty mixed up. For both of us." He waited until she looked at him again before continuing. "We still need to talk. We need to come up with a way to get a confession out of Miller." Nick refrained from mentioning Doc Abbott. It was there between them, but he was as reluctant to end the harmony of their morning as she had been. Ignoring that, he plowed on. "What do you think Miller really wants from you?" Willa sighed and resolved to concentrate on the discussion at hand. *Silly fool*, she chided herself. This morning may have been memorable, and very informative for her, but she couldn't forget that it was Nick's life they were dealing with and that *that* was the most important thing to him.

"I don't know," she answered honestly. "But I agree that his joining my program probably isn't coincidence. He acted very different last night from what I'd seen in the past. He was very moody, almost paranoid." She turned to look out the window, embarrassed again over her continuing naïveté where Eric was concerned. "Nick, I think he was snorting coke right in the club. I didn't figure it out until later. And during dinner he hinted that a relationship with him would be mutually rewarding." She turned back to face him. "Do you know what he meant?"

Nick's eyes narrowed dangerously. He avoided her question, asking one of his own. "What kind of relationship?"

Willa wondered if she had imagined the almost proprietary look that had flashed across his face. "I won't deny that he wants to resume our old relationship." Nick remained quiet, but she sensed his patience was nearing an end.

"Nick?" she said, concerned when his attention appeared to be drifting. "I told him we could be friends and that our training sessions would give us plenty of time to talk."

"He accepted that? What happened to his bounding confidence?" Nick asked almost absently, still frowning over her previous comment.

Willa was confused. Did Nick actually expect her to continue dating Eric after the scene in the parking lot? "I didn't give him much choice," she answered evenly. "That's not to say he'll give up. Knowing him, he'll probably push his case every chance he gets. But I've thought about it a lot, and I really think I can find out what you need to know and still keep it strictly professional."

Agitated when Nick continued to frown, Willa leaned over and grabbed his arm to get his full attention, ignoring completely the jolt that coming into contact with him always seemed to produce. "I will do just about anything to clear your name. But I will not date Eric Miller," she stated very clearly. "He makes me very uncomfortable. Besides, I think my idea will work."

"I agree," Nick responded calmly in the face of her outburst. Her attitude firmly cemented his decision to keep her in the dark about the planted drugs. That left only one remaining obstacle.

Nick shifted in his seat to face her, using her hand that was still gripping his arm as leverage to tug her closer. "I know we should wait until this episode is over"—his voice softened and a flicker of vulnerability showed on his face—"but somehow I don't think I can."

His velvety voice stroked Willa's senses until she felt like purring. The tiny trace of uncertainty melted her already softened resistance. But her pride and her confidence were still rather battered, and she had to know. "Why?"

"I wish I knew," Nick said softly. More clearly he said, "I can't ignore, or just shut off, what's happening between us."

"Nick, I can't—"

"I know. Neither can I." He closed the distance between them, slanting his lips across hers in a hard, fast, passion-filled kiss, then abruptly broke contact and set her gently away—a habit that was beginning to annoy the daylights out of her.

Gripping the door handle, she had to clear her throat twice before her voice lost its throaty whisper. "Nick, I—" He turned at the thready sound of her voice. "Let me finish this time, will you?"

That comment earned her a flash of his lethal

grin, making her pulse soar. "I agree that there is something going on here besides proving you were framed." She held up her hand when he started to come closer. "But I also agree that we should wait until this is over before exploring it."

"I think I just proved why that won't work," he said, still smiling. "I can't separate my feelings into neat little compartments, Willa. This is all intertwined. We'll explore this . . . thing and clear my name at the same time."

Willa wasn't sure whom he was trying harder to convince. It bothered her to disregard her instincts to trust him, but her instincts had a rotten track record and the deep dark truth was she just couldn't be sure what his true motives were. Still, she was forced to admit that Nick had come to mean a lot to her in the short time they'd known each other. A whole lot.

But the little devil on her shoulder kept whispering doubts. *Does he just want to run the course of his mutual chemistry so he can get you out of his system?*

Nick sensed she was battling her demons and let the topic drop. For now. Willa might not want to admit it, he assured himself, but she could no more ignore what was going on between them than he could. But she'd soon figure that out. "When is Miller's training appointment?"

"Monday. Monday morning at ten."

"Do you think you'd be up to talking to him—later?" Willa turned swiftly, her eyes questioning his intent. "Be realistic," he hastily added. "He's too smart to say anything incriminating with other people around to overhear. All I'm suggesting is that you arrange to talk with him after work."

Slack-jawed and flushed with anger, Willa couldn't believe what she was hearing. It hurt—terribly—to realize she'd misjudged him so badly. Nick didn't really care about her at all. "Didn't you hear anything I just said?" Too angry and hurt to let him answer, her temper took over. "Don't get me wrong, Nick. I hate what Eric did to you. I hate what he did to me. But if he's as sneaky and conniving as you say he is, then how can you ask me to go off alone with him again?"

Nick immediately grabbed her flailing arm and pulled it down until her clenched fist rested on his knee. "You won't be alone with him, Willa. I'll be there, and so will Sky."

She was completely confused, and all the fight went out of her. "Correct me if I'm wrong, but what in the hell makes you think he'll talk if *you're* there?"

Nick scrubbed his hand over his face, frustration at his inept handling of the matter warring with the guilt he felt for putting her into such a position. "I never intended for you to leave the club. My idea is to get him into your office. We'll rig the security camera, hide it somehow, and record him."

"Won't work." Willa understood his plan and ignored all the painful implications of Nick's priorities and how far he was willing to go to get the information he needed.

"Why not?"

"The monitor doesn't record voices. Won't you need to have his comments on tape for the police to believe you?"

Nick breathed a sigh of relief. She was going to do it! "So we'll plant a recorder somewhere. I doubt Eric suspects that I'm on to him, but seeing me has probably put him on guard. Still, he needs you for something. As you said, his coming back into your life isn't coincidence."

Nick didn't have to remind her that Eric wasn't back because he truly felt anything for her. And she'd do well to remember Nick hadn't entered her life for that reason either. "All right. I'll set it up with him tomorrow morning. Who is going to do all this fancy wiring and planting and rigging?"

Nick wanted to kiss her for what she'd agreed to put herself through for him. He didn't. He knew from her reactions and her very expressive face that he was still walking a tightrope with her over gaining her complete trust. He couldn't keep the broad grin from slashing across his face, however. "No problem. Sky and I will figure something out."

Willa smiled back, wishing she was better at resisting that teasing grin. "I really have to get in to work for a bit. Can we figure the rest of this out later?"

"Sure, I'll follow you back and talk with Sky. Anything else we need to go over we can discuss at lunch tomorrow."

"Lunch?" Willa raised an eyebrow over his controlling tactics, congratulating herself for still having some spine left. "Sorry, I can't. With the program starting tomorrow, I figured I'd grab a bite at the club between appointments. We can go over it during your session tomorrow."

Nick was shaking his head before she finished. "We will have lunch." He ignored the expression on her face and the threatening explosion of temper. He knew he'd pushed her pretty far today, but on this issue he wasn't going to back down. "Willa, I know you. You'll get busy and forget. You're going to need to be alert tomorrow night."

His reminder of the disgraceful way she'd

fainted in the parking lot was less than gentle-manly, she thought. "I've been taking care of myself for a long time, Nick Logan. If I say I'll eat lunch, I'll eat lunch. And I don't need you holding my hand."

"I'm taking you to lunch, Willa." His smile broadened. It occurred to him that taking care of her was never going to be easy, but in that instant he knew he'd always try anyway. He reached for her hand to prevent his already high doctor bills from escalating. "Besides," he went on, lacing his fingers through hers and squeezing lightly, "I like holding your hand. And I can't talk to you during my session since it won't be with you."

Willa tried again to yank her hand away, but he held on. "Okay, why won't you be at your session tomorrow?"

He ignored her. "Does what's-his-name work tomorrow?"

She felt dazed and could answer only "What's-his-name who?"

"You know, the gym flunky you tried to pawn me off on when I first told you I wanted you as a trainer."

"You mean Richard soon-to-be-Dr. Thorn-ton?"

"A doctor, huh?" Nick pretended to give it

serious thought. "Well, I'm sure he's not your professional equal, but I guess he'll do."

"Thank you, sir," Willa responded, inordinately pleased over his lighthearted compliment. "Now, may I ask why you need Richard?"

"Sure." Before Willa could react, Nick reached over, weaving his hand under her hair, and pulled her across the seat. His eyes remained open; Willa's did as well. He kissed her, slowly at first, and when Willa's eyes drifted shut, he deepened the kiss on a groan.

Before he lost his head, certain the rest of his anatomy would quickly follow, he broke contact. Except with her hair. He wound one of her burnished curls around his finger and dipped his mouth to hers again, amazed that the first taste had him at the edge of losing control. Only a car pulling into the space next to theirs broke them apart. "We both know this isn't going to wait."

Willa just nodded, too affected by his kiss and by his words to respond otherwise. She grabbed the door handle and pulled hard, taking the lifeline that fate had thrown her. Fate being fickle, she knew she might not get another one.

Only after Willa was safely out of his arms and in her car did Nick acknowledge the clutch in his gut when she'd agreed to put herself directly in Miller's path again.

As he followed her back to Millennium he decided no matter what happened, he wouldn't ask any more of her. And he'd find another way to deal with Doc—perhaps Sky could get Box to rig the camera for them. That would give Nick a chance to ask Box if he'd be willing to do some digging into Doc's personal business. Maybe find a clue as to why he'd helped Miller in the first place.

SEVEN

Willa slapped another pile of folders on her desk and took a second to down another cup of coffee. As proud as she was that her training program had officially begun, she briefly wished she could have stayed home this morning. As a rule, Mondays weren't her favorite days, but this one had been deliciously different.

Nick had shown up bright and early with a bag of groceries and a sexy grin. Apparently he'd taken his self-appointed role as her nutritional counselor to heart. His excuse was that he wanted to give her moral support for the big day. She decided she had enough to worry over, so she simply accepted his gesture at face value rather than give herself another headache by trying to dissect it for ulterior motives. Besides, he cooked a mean omelet.

Scooping up the phone in one hand and balancing folders in the other, she answered, "What now, Kelly? All my afternoon appointments canceled?"

"Sorry, boss," answered the rough-hewn voice on the other end. "Been a tough one, huh?"

"Sky! Yeah, it has." *And it's about to get tougher.*

"Hey, you should be proud. The new program is going like gangbusters. Have you heard from Nick?"

Willa debated whether Sky knew about their shared breakfast. "Not recently," she answered, hedging.

"Well, Kelly told me his appointment with Richard is for three this afternoon. I wondered—"

"He's meeting me here for lunch after Eric's session. Do you want to join us?"

"No, no. I just wanted to double-check with him about the stuff we rigged in your office last night. Have you checked it all out?"

She glanced at the leafy plant on her shelf, unable to see the lens tucked inside, but knowing it was there based on her earlier inspection. "Yeah. I guess we're all set. All that's left is for me to convince Eric to talk."

"You can do it, Willa." Sky was silent for a moment. When he spoke again, his voice had an even rougher edge than usual. "Nick isn't always real good with telling people how he feels. If it weren't for him, I'd probably be in some rehab program myself—and not for a physical injury, if you get my drift. He helped me through a rough time, helped me out when everyone else had given up on me. I guess what I'm trying to say is that when Nick believes in someone, he stands by that person. He believes in you, Willa."

"Thanks, Sky. He has a pretty good friend in you too. After all, you stood by him when no one else would."

"Yeah, well, I'd do more than that if I could. He won't say it, but he's counting on you. Thanks for believing in him too."

Willa hung up and turned to leave—and face Eric. With Sky's warm words of encouragement echoing in her ears, she felt a new sense of strength. A few minutes later she strolled into the training room, chin lifted and ready.

Several hours later Nick found Willa in her office, bent over a stack of folders. "Hi, Princess. How'd it go?"

Willa's head snapped up in surprise. She hadn't even heard him enter. "Hi, yourself. Fine. He'll be here after closing to 'reminisce about the good old days.'"

Nick rested his cane on the visitor's chair and leaned a hip on the corner of her desk, careful not to dislodge the precarious towers of folders stacked everywhere. "Looks like you're a success." When she only smiled weakly in response, he cut the chatter. "What did he say about the other night, anything?"

"Oh yeah, he was just full of remorse." She smiled sarcastically as she remembered how Eric had flashed his forgive-me-I'm-famous smile and fully expected all to be forgiven. "I think he was more worried about the possibility of a nasty tabloid account of our date than anything else."

Nick noticed the lines of strain feathering the edges of her eyes and bracketing her mouth. Without conscious thought he reached across the desk and smoothed a rough-tipped finger as gently as he could over the drawn skin, not stopping until it warmed under his caress. "Thank you, Willa. I know this isn't easy, but with any luck, it will all be over soon."

Willa snorted. "Please, don't put your faith in my luck or we're doomed before we begin."

Nick simply smiled and tapped a finger against her bottom lip. "Don't be so hard on yourself. I think your luck is about to change."

Her stomach chose that moment to announce its presence, loudly protesting its current empty state. Nick grinned and reached for her hand, drawing her up and guiding her around the desk until she came to stand before him. He released her hand and gently gripped her hips, pulling her between his legs. "Remind me to bring some bread and butter with me next time."

Nick watched with fascination as Willa's eyes slowly darkened. The becoming glow spreading slowly across her cheeks gave him the distinct impression that he was her preferred lunch menu. "Keep looking at me like that, and I'm liable to think I'm the blue-plate special." He chuckled when the glow turned into a deeper crimson. Lord, she was fun to tease. He gently nudged her away until they were both standing. "Let's get out of here for a while. You've more than earned the break. Fresh air would do us both good. What do you say?"

Her gaze fastened on his lips as he spoke and he couldn't resist a brief kiss. But one touch was not enough, and the light caress turned into a powerful kiss.

She swallowed hard when he pulled away. "I'd say we're wasting time."

Her voice was brandy laced with pure sex. "Kissing you will never be wasted time." He wanted her so badly that if he didn't get her out in the public eye in the next sixty seconds, her office floor would be a likely destination for them both. "Let's go."

He caught her hand and scooped up his cane, hauling them both to the door. Just before opening it, he turned suddenly, bringing her hard up against him. He smiled down into her face. "You know something? You're one hell of a woman." He underscored his words with a long drugging kiss that left them gasping for air. When he could, he said, "I know a great place nearby. The food's okay and the service can't be beat."

Willa's stomach answered before she could form a word, and they both laughed. "I guess I don't have a choice."

Nick's smile turned wicked. "I was wondering when you'd figure that out."

Willa didn't start to guess his choice of restaurant until they left the commercial area of Tysons Corner and headed west on Route 7. When Nick turned into a residential area, she knew something was up. When she glanced at Nick, the innocent smile on his face answered her unasked question.

"I didn't know you lived in Reston," she said pointedly.

"You never asked," he responded, flashing

her his thigh-melting grin. He gestured at the large tree-filled lots. "It's as close as I could get to living in the woods and still avoid a long drive to practice."

Willa glanced sharply at Nick. This was the first time he'd referred to his recent career without sounding bitter. She really wanted to discuss it with him, but wasn't sure how to approach the subject without causing him any more pain.

She turned her attention out her window as he made several turns, winding deeper into the forest of homes, which would be almost invisible, hidden behind the dense spring foliage in another month or so. "I know you must miss your career. After you clear your name, will you go back to football?"

Nick's gaze remained focused on the road, but his smile faded somewhat. "Because of the ban, I didn't play at all last season. I tried to get reinstated a few days ago, but the commissioner wasn't convinced. The case being dismissed didn't prove my innocence, as the public made so vocally clear. Even so, the commissioner had based his decision on the fact that I was the only team member to fail the mandatory drug test."

"Can't you just take another test?"

Nick's laughter was more of a bark and lacked any humor. "I have. Twice. Aced them both." His tone turned sarcastic. "All that earned me was a pat on the back from the commissioner and my coach for doing so well at staying clean. Of course, it's not a particularly tough accomplishment," he added bitterly, "when you've never done drugs in your life."

She heard the blows to his pride and the enormity of his loss underlying each word he had spoken. "I'm so sorry, Nick. It's all so unfair," she said, her voice hoarse with unshed tears. "What happens next?"

"That's for the commissioner to decide." Nick pulled into a winding, tree-lined driveway, then glanced over at Willa. "If everything works out, and I prove my innocence, I hope he'll lift the ban. Otherwise I'll be judged on my ability to test clean until the end of next season." He pulled in front of a cedar and fieldstone house nestled in a grove of oak trees and parked next to a bright red Jeep Eagle.

Willa placed her hand on his arm as he started to open the door. "You know, another man might simply wait out the year, test clean, and use that as his revenge. But there's more at stake for you than your pride, isn't there? I mean, no one wants to be thought of as a drug dealer or user, but I get the impression this goes deeper than changing the average citizen's opinion of you."

Nick looked up sharply at her words, his defenses lowered for a split second, revealing that she'd scored a direct hit.

"It's because of the kids, isn't it?" she asked softly. "The kids at the camp."

Nick nodded brusquely, shifting his gaze as if something outside of the car had just snagged his attention. After a moment he said, "I try to tell myself it doesn't matter. But it does." Willa ran her hand up his arm until it rested on his shoulder. He turned to look at her, finding the tender gesture matched the look in her eyes. The feelings she inspired swirled inside him. He wanted to spill his guts. He wanted to hold her, touch her, kiss her. He loved her.

Clearing his throat to dislodge the lump that had formed there, he also cleared his mind and concentrated on answering her. "I started several summers ago. The coach has run the camp for a long time and always asks the team to volunteer some time. At first I did it for the coach. I have to admit that at first I didn't think a week or two away from crime and peer pressure could make that much difference to the kids."

"But it did help, didn't it?" Her tone made the question more of a statement.

"Yeah, believe it or not. At the least it kept them off the streets."

"And off drugs."

Nick raised his eyebrows, and a smile teased the edges of his mouth. "That too. Don't ask me why they listened to me. My background couldn't have been more different from theirs. Sometimes I think I learned more from them."

"You were a role model to them."

Nick shrugged. "I'm just a guy who loves football and happens to play it fairly well. The media likes to hype that up. A few good seasons and, bam, you're a role model."

"They couldn't have picked a better one as far as I'm concerned," Willa defended staunchly. She could have sworn his face actually reddened. "My dad didn't really talk about that part much. It must have been tough, though. That's a big responsibility to carry around."

Nick gazed at her intently for another second, then went on. "It is—was. But I remember how I worshiped players as a kid. Dreaming of being one of them was what fueled my desire and helped me achieve my goal of becoming a pro."

"And so you took the advantage that being a public figure gives you to help the kids at the summer camp."

Nick nodded. "I can't seem to stop thinking how I would have felt if something like this had happened to one of my heroes. I mean, I'm no hero, but—"

"But you were to those kids." Willa couldn't prevent the intense pride she felt for him from shining in her eyes. "Do you still want to play? After all of this?"

"At first, after my arrest, that's all I thought about. But lately I don't know. I'm not so sure anymore. I'm thirty-two, which is old for a player, especially one with my history of injuries." He pushed himself out of the car. "I probably would have retired in the next year or two. I just wanted to do it on my terms."

Willa climbed out on her side of the car and met up with Nick in front of it. "What will you do?"

Nick was warmed by the real caring she exhibited. He hadn't missed her quick assessment of his house and was amused by her apparent concern about her ability to maintain his lifestyle. And the fact that she hadn't shown a trace of suspicion as to how he might be earning an income these days wasn't lost on him—or his heart.

A slow smile spread across his face; his blue eyes were twinkling. He picked up Willa's hand, weaving his fingers through hers, and walked to the arched front door. "What I'm going to do is take you inside, show off my culinary skills, such as they are, and talk about anything except football."

Nick let the door swing open on its own and tipped her chin up until their eyes met. "Hey, Princess, you okay?"

No! she wanted to shout. *I think I'm falling in love with you.* Only her pride kept her from blurting it out. His life, his pain, was her first priority, and that precluded burdening him with that sort of declaration. "You know me." She laughed weakly. "A few hours without food and I get wacky."

Nick's eyes narrowed in suspicion. He rubbed his thumb over her bottom lip, then lowered his lips to hers.

Willa responded to his gentle touch like a flower to the strong rays of the sun. She blossomed under his probing tongue, opening her mouth to his, loving the warm taste of him. It wasn't until she placed her hands on his chest for support, her knees melting like butter left in the sun, that she realized the full extent of his restraint.

Nick's heart was pounding so hard she could feel the vibrations trip over her skin until her pulse matched his. He leaned back against the doorframe, pulling her more tightly into his arms, and accidentally pressed the doorbell.

"I don't know about you," he said roughly, touching his nose to hers, "but I've never heard bells before."

Relaxing back against him on a helpless laugh, she said, "At least it wasn't my stomach growling this time."

He laughed deeply, naturally, and it was a marvelous transformation. Willa noted the crinkles at the corner of his eyes and the hint of a dimple in his cheek. All signs of a man who had once laughed easily and often.

Until eight months ago.

"What brought on that frown?" Nick gazed at her lips, wanting to smooth the soft skin with his tongue until her smile reappeared. "Don't answer that. Obviously our ten minutes are up." He pulled her inside, into a large tiled foyer. "Wanna join me in the kitchen and help with lunch?"

Willa said yes, shamelessly willing to put their problems aside, even if only for a short while. Adopting a mock look of disdain, she said, "When you said this place had good service, I didn't realize the service was going to be me."

Nick bit back a comment, content to let her off with a kiss. Short and sweet though it was, he still barely dragged his mouth from hers before the flames of passion could scorch his good intentions. "At least I had faith in you. I could have said the service was lousy, you know."

"How do you know it won't be?" His sexy smile made it easy to tease back. Determined to have the last word for a change, she brushed past him. She found the well-equipped kitchen easily, glancing enviously at the cozy breakfast nook tucked into a large bay window. Catching the reflection of her smile in the glass, she was struck by how much and how truly she was enjoying herself.

That realization made it easier to push aside all her questions about what their future might or might not hold.

Nick moved slowly, enjoying the opportunity to appreciate Willa's well-toned backside. Willa was wearing black fitted trousers with an emerald-green polo shirt that had the club's emblem stitched into the breast pocket. He'd noticed that emblem right away. He mentally added polo shirts to his growing list of erotic attire. By the time he reached the kitchen, he headed straight for the coldest appliance in the room. Glancing inside the stainless-steel refrigerator, he said, "I'm sure I have enough in here to whip up a decent sandwich. Or would you rather have salad?" He turned to look at Willa, who was wandering around the room, more interested in the various antique cooking implements hanging on the walls than in sizing up the financial ramifications of his high-tech appliances. He was struck by how at home she looked.

She turned and caught him staring. Nick felt his entire body tighten at the obvious desire in her eyes. Desire that had nothing to do with his profession or his income. It was bad enough that he kept picturing her upstairs in his bed, her wild curls spread across his pillowcase. . . . He quickly looked back at the contents of the fridge, the cold blast of air doing little to cool his overheated imagination.

"Don't go to any trouble. I'm sure I'll like whatever you want." Willa swore she heard him groan. "Nick?" His head was deep into the recesses of the refrigerator, and while it gave her a great view of his buns, Willa wondered what on earth he was doing.

"I have some soda if you want," came his muffled offer. He finally pulled his head out. "Or I could make iced tea."

"Water with some ice will be fine," she answered cautiously, trying to figure out why he was acting so oddly. When he just smiled and nodded, she shrugged it off as her imagination working overtime. Willa turned her attention back to

Nick's unusual decorations. "Where did you find all these old tools?"

"Some belonged to my folks. The rest I picked up at auctions."

"You like to go to auctions?" she asked in surprise.

"Is that so unusual?"

"Yes. I mean, no. It's just that I didn't picture you as a connoisseur of antiques."

"Athletes have been known to possess some refinement." He turned to face her. "We're not all dumb jocks."

"I didn't mean to imply that you were lacking in intelligence. And I'd be the last one to—"

"I know, I know," Nick broke in, his voice gentler now. "I'm sorry, Willa. It's just that after years of putting up with the media's constant stereotyping of athletes, I guess I get a little testy." When Willa raised her eyebrows at his use of the word "little," Nick added, "Anyway, a few rusty kitchen implements hardly qualify me as a connoisseur of anything."

"Rusty or new, would you happen to have a clock?"

"What? Oh, don't worry, we have plenty of time."

"It's not that. I just wanted to make sure we

hadn't broken the ten-minute limit between arguments."

"Or kisses." Nick fought the urge to drag her upstairs to his bed.

All that talk about refinement and all you can think about is Neanderthal lovemaking tactics. Nick turned back to the counter and started slicing tomatoes and ham, all the while debating the wisdom of handling sharp knives while in the same room with Willa. He glanced again at her. He was thinking how great she looked in his kitchen, wondering how much greater she'd look in his bed. Could he actually be contemplating the whole ring-on-the-finger routine? Especially with the very woman who'd helped create the mess in the first place?

Nick dropped ice into two glass tumblers and filled them with water. *I've just been celibate too long. Maybe if I spread that beautiful hair across the sheets for real, I'd get over this.*

He'd tried to convince himself of that the past few nights when he was alone in bed, hard with wanting her. But with her in person, in the cold light of day, he wondered if a lifetime spent in her arms would be enough.

He carried the plates to the table, realizing as he watched her that darkness wasn't a prerequisite for getting hard, and sat down before he attracted Willa's attention to his arousal.

"I wish I had a bay window in my kitchen." She smiled briefly at him before taking her seat. "You said something about being in the woods again. Where did you live before?"

"I was raised in Vermont. Not that Virginia is similar, but I feel closer to Vermont somehow when I'm surrounded by trees." Nick's face took on a faraway look. "Who knows, maybe when this is all over, I'll move back north."

Almost choking on her sandwich, Willa still forced herself to take note of his use of the word "I." The mere thought of him moving far away was physically painful, but however much it hurt, she accepted the fact that her fantasy of happy-ever-after would remain just that. A fantasy. He'd all but told her straight out there would be no "us" after his name was cleared. But she'd deal with that harsh truth later. Her feelings for Nick ran deeper than she'd ever imagined possible, and foolish or not, she desperately wanted whatever time they had left.

Silence descended over the small table, but the desire between them fairly screamed as they picked at their food. Nick gave up trying to eat when he realized he'd systematically taken all the poppy seeds off his roll.

As if by silent agreement, Willa and Nick started to clear away the few dishes. Their hands brushed and the charged atmosphere intensified a few thousand watts. Willa moved her hand away, but Nick grabbed it, holding it until she looked up at him. "It never ceases to amaze me how simply touching you can affect me so much." Holding her hand, he moved around the table, until barely an inch separated them.

"Nick, I . . ."

"Ding," he whispered. "Our ten minutes are definitely up." He closed the distance between them and pressed her back against the round oak table, then kissed her.

Her taste, the texture of her lips, the sweet smell of her enthralled him. When she deepened the kiss, his fingers began to tremble from the effort of restraint. She turned her head slightly, moaning softly as he took the invitation and continued his sensual assault along the soft line of her jaw, trailing tender kisses to the collar of her shirt.

"Willa." He groaned against her heated skin. "I want you. More than I've ever wanted anyone or anything in my life." He summoned his strength and pulled back to look at her. It was a calculated risk, because the look on her face would decide the fate of their relationship.

Her lips parted slightly as she choked back a

soft gasp, and he was a goner. He wrapped his arms around her, molding her to him, unable to decide whether he'd won or lost.

His kisses dipped to the opening at the front of her shirt; his hands slid up to cup her breasts, kneading them softly until she thought she'd scream from the need he'd created in her. She gasped, letting go of the table and weaving her fingers through the jumble of dark hair curling against his neck. She reveled in the feel of him and took full advantage of the knowledge that for now, she alone had the right to touch him, taste him.

For the first time Willa knew real lovemaking. An equal sharing of each other. Nick would share his body with her and demand she do the same. He would take precious care of the gift of her body—but what would he do with her heart?

She felt her shirt being tugged from her pants and a second later Nick's lips grazed her nipples through the lace of her bra. And she realized that Nick Logan was as necessary to her survival as the air she breathed.

Her decision made, she let go, allowing her intense sensations to guide her. She quickly grew impatient to be as close to him as she could be. She wanted to melt into him, fuse her body with his. She drew his face to hers and kissed him, watching him closely as she told him with her lips and tongue that she would be an equal partner in this seduction. Suddenly kissing him wasn't enough; she needed to touch his skin as he'd touched hers, taste him as he'd tasted her. She pulled at his shirt, swearing softly at the fabric that hindered her goal.

"You do have a colorful way with words, Red." Nick chuckled against her skin.

"I, uh, guess princesses don't swear at a time like this, do they?"

Nick's teasing smile turned tender, her lightly spoken words unable to cover her vulnerability. "Your response to me is beautiful and honest. How could I ever want more?"

He kissed her deeply, thoroughly, showing her just how strongly she affected him. Feathering kisses over her eyelids and cheekbones, he finally groaned and buried his face in her hair. "Willa, if you don't tell me to stop now, in a minute I may not be able to." This time he didn't have the nerve to look at her face. He was too stunned by the depth of his need for her to say yes.

Willa loosened her fingers still twisted in his shirt, letting them trail slowly across her shoulders. She pushed gently until she could look in his eyes. "I want to make love with you, Nick Logan." Her green eyes sparkled, defenses gone, imploring him.

"You sure about this, Princess?"

In a sultry tone she added, "Please hurry, you don't want to waste your ten minutes."

Nick's smile turned downright predatory. "I'm going to need a hell of a lot longer than ten minutes to love you the way I want to."

EIGHT

Nick led the way back to the foyer. He held only her hand as they went up the stairs, afraid if he touched any more of her, they might not make it up the entire flight. As they reached the door to the master bedroom, he turned to her, needing to make sure she hadn't had a change of heart.

Pure desire, and something else he was afraid to examine too closely, shone like a beacon in her eyes, welcoming him in from the solitary storm he'd battled for almost a year.

In that moment he knew he'd been fooling himself if he thought that once was ever going to be enough.

Bright sunshine poured through the blinds, but Willa's only impression of Nick's bedroom was from sunbeams playing across the midnight-blue bedspread, highlighting the waves of his dark hair as he sat on the edge of the king-size bed, pulling her down on top of him. After that, everything became hazy.

As one, they slowly rolled to their sides, their gazes locked as tightly as their embrace. Willa trusted Nick with her heart, knowing that making love with him would be as special and unique as the bond they shared.

And it was love. Pure, if not simple.

She made a weak attempt to mask the depth of her feelings, but Nick was staring at her so intently, his eyes mirroring the desire in hers, she abandoned all pretense. He pulled her closer, the strength of his desire pressing against her belly. Confronted with his very real response to her, she was unable to suppress a delighted smile.

A slow, lazy grin spread across Nick's face. They might have only a short time together, but he was obviously not about to rush things. "Want to let me in on the reason for that sultry little smile?" He reached out, twining a curl around his finger.

"Sultry? I don't think I've ever been sultry."

"Trust me. You could give lessons on being sultry to a New Orleans summer." Nick punctuated his statement with a kiss on each corner of her mouth. "All this talk of heat is making me feel way overdressed. You?"

"Uh-huh." Any doubts she had about being nervous with Nick vanished. His gentle teasing and slow, seductive smiles were guaranteed to keep her right there with him. She shifted back to pull off her shirt when he stopped her.

"I was kind of looking forward to doing that." His expression was priceless and Willa knew then that he'd never be satisfied until she was. A concept Eric had been light-years away from understanding.

Letting go of the last of the demons and doubts Eric had so expertly woven into her mind, she practiced that sultry smile again. "So was I."

"You're trying to burn me alive with those green eyes, aren't you? Why don't I work on getting you naked, and if we still have any strength left when I'm done, you can return the favor." Willa's eyes widened at his suggestion, revealing how little she knew about playing in bed, and Nick felt his heart fill so tightly he thought it would burst with the tenderness he felt for her. "Just follow my lead, and I promise we'll both have fun."

Willa nodded, too busy biting her bottom lip as he bent to nudge the hem of her shirt with his nose, trailing his tongue over her stomach as he worked it slowly back over her breasts, to say anything.

"You're perfect. I knew you would be." Nick's hoarse whisper fanned across her skin as he traced the swirling design on her silk bra with his tongue, watching her nipples create a new pattern under the exotic print. He slowly drew back the emerald lace trim that pressed into her skin, strained by the growing fullness of her breasts.

Willa gasped as the cool air caressed her newly bared skin. Nick pulled the dusky beaded tips into his mouth, gently sucking each one in turn. She arched into him, needing more. She reached out to him, needing to feel the warmth of his skin, assure herself that this was real.

"Uh-uh," he murmured against her soft skin. "My turn first, you promised." He pushed at her hand, held it gently beside her head until he was sure she would keep it there, then returned his attention to the waistband of her slacks. "Just relax."

"But I want you to feel this way, too."

"Then you have no idea how much this is turning me on. Believe me, I am supremely happy. In a perfect world, I'd stay right here, tasting you, touching you, all day." Nick smiled at her, loving the way her pupils dilated even further with every suggestive comment he made. Dear Lord, he was going to enjoy opening her up to the knowledge of how wonderful lovemaking could be. He winked at her, then bent his head to her zipper. He lowered it with one hand, then looking at her, he put his finger in his mouth and traced the outside edge of her belly button with it.

Willa arched against the damp roughness of his finger. She'd never thought of her navel as an erogenous zone before, but as he dipped his tongue into the slight depression, she experienced a rush of moist heat between her legs that was almost painful. "Nick, I . . ."

"What, Willa? Tell me what you want."

What she wanted was for him to bury himself inside her deep enough to extinguish the flames licking at her core. But she couldn't say that to him, not yet. "I want"—she broke off to clear the rough edges from her throat—"I want my turn now."

Nick rolled her pants down to her hips. "Let me take these off first." He slid them the rest of the way off, then turned and pulled himself across the bed to lie beside her, trailing a hand along her body as he moved. "I barely got started, you know."

Willa didn't answer, she was already working at his shirt. He cheated by pulling it over his head for her. She didn't mind. She was too busy staring at each sculpted ridge of his body. She lifted a tentative hand, wanting to touch him everywhere at once and not knowing where to begin.

"Touch me, Willa." He pressed her hand over his heart and their eyes met. Her fingers felt the rapid pulse beneath his skin. "Yeah, it amazes me too. All that from just a look. Now tell me what I taste like, Willa."

Unable to resist, she lowered her head and swirled her tongue against his nipple. It pebbled immediately and Nick groaned. She looked up to find him staring at her so fiercely that she wondered what she'd done wrong. "You okay?"

"You really want to know? Ask me what I want, Willa. I'm not too shy to tell you."

Willa swallowed hard. His voice was like gravel, a rasp so low it vibrated across his skin. He wanted her. Badly. The very idea thrilled her as much as it frightened her. He must have seen it in her expression because he pushed up onto one elbow and tilted her chin up with his other hand.

"Am I making you nervous?"

"No."

"Don't lie, Willa. Do you want me to stop talking?"

She looked him straight in the eye. "No."

"Then take my pants off before they won't come off."

Her hands trembled badly as she unsnapped

his jeans. She couldn't have prevented the moan from escaping her lips if she'd tried when she discovered that nothing came between Nick and his Levi's. "You're beautiful."

"Hey, that's my line." He flopped back on the bed, groaning as she pulled his jeans off and tossed them on the floor.

"Does your knee hurt?"

"I wouldn't know. I can't feel anything below my—"

"Nick!"

"Willa!" he mimicked. He smiled gently when she looked up at him. "Come here." He pulled her over his body, groaning into her hair as his erection rubbed against her belly. "Do you want me inside you as badly as I need to be there?"

Willa nodded slowly, admitting to herself that she was beginning to like the way Nick talked in bed. It took some getting used to after Eric's grunting directions and sighed disappointment— but she could soon become addicted to his provocative verbal foreplay. "You're incorrigible, you know that?"

"I think the word you're looking for is corruptible."

"So, corrupt me and I'll corrupt you."

Nick let out a shout of approval and rolled

over, pinning her beneath him. "I knew we were made for each other."

Willa's smile faded and her heart began pounding so hard she couldn't hear. More than anything she wanted that to be true. " Love me, Nick."

Nick growled low in his throat and captured her lips in a soul-searing kiss. He moved between her legs, pressing against her, then stopped. Abruptly he rolled back over and pushed up to sit at the edge of the bed, Willa straddling his lap.

"Nick?"

"Wrap your legs around me." Nick twitched involuntarily, his need for her intense. "I think I'm gonna die. Reach behind you and grab one of those packets."

Willa picked up the condom and handed it to him.

Nick merely looked at her.

"You want me to . . ."

"I believe in sharing the responsibility of birth control."

Willa caught the twinkle in his eyes and smiled herself. She fumbled with the packet, her fingers too shaky to get a grip on the slippery plastic.

Nick took it from her, tore it open, and

gently lay back on the bed, shifting her off to his side. "Hurry, or it will be over before we begin."

She rolled it along the length of him, barely finishing before he pulled her under him and nestled between her thighs. She automatically wrapped her legs around his lean waist, instinctively rising to meet him.

"Are you ready for me?"

"I think I've always been ready for you."

Nick kissed her soft and deep as he pushed slowly into her. His biceps bunched under the strain of keeping himself from plunging. "So hot. So tight." He let out a slow moan as he eased more deeply into her. "So mine."

Unable to keep his body from establishing a faster rhythm, he began to move inside her. He reveled in the intensity of their lovemaking as she matched him thrust for thrust. All too soon she drove him to the edge. "Willa, I can't . . ." His words died as he clenched his jaw and drove as deeply into her as he could in his release.

As soon as he stopped shuddering, he rolled to his side, keeping her with him. He buried his face in her hair. "I am so sorry. I promise I'll make it up to you."

Willa was still too awed by the force of his powerful body filling hers to understand what in the world he was talking about. When his words finally sank in, she reached for his face, turning his head to hers. "Do you mean it could actually be any better?"

Nick's mouth dropped open, then quickly snapped shut as a devilish smile carved a tiny dimple into his cheek. "Oh, yeah, Princess. It gets a whole lot better."

He swept her into his arms and began a slow assault on her mouth. By the time he'd reached her breasts, she was writhing beneath him. His mouth dipped lower, touching off sparks as he nibbled around her belly button. "Nick, please."

"Please what?"

"I need. . . . I—"

"This?" Nick slowly tucked his tongue into the moisture between her legs. He was rewarded with a gasp as her hips surged forward, pressing more intimately against him.

Willa felt like she'd just stepped off the edge of an active volcano. Nothing in her limited experience had ever prepared her for this. The need for release was so great that hot tears seeped from under her closed eyelashes. She must have whimpered because Nick stopped abruptly.

"Am I hurting you?"

"Please don't stop now or I'll die."

His laugh was so provocative she arched her hips again. "A knight would never leave his damsel in such obvious distress." He touched her again, but she wriggled away, pushing at his shoulders.

"What's wrong, baby?"

"I don't know. I'm so close to . . . Nick? I need you inside me."

He would have thought it impossible, but those softly spoken words, so achingly vulnerable yet beautifully strong, accomplished in seconds what should have taken an hour.

He pulled her on top of him, gripping her hips, and they quickly established a rhythm that was both universal and uniquely theirs.

It couldn't possibly get any better.

She was wonderfully wrong.

Willa moved over him in a wanton abandon that would have shocked her only a few hours before. It felt perfect. He felt perfect. She ran her hands over his chest and shoulders, gripping his powerful biceps as he bucked against her. The heady combination of their passion, intertwined with the intense desire to please each other, proved to be a powerful force of nature. As Nick moved he touched off a coil of heat that slowly started to spiral—winding tighter and tighter in her body until she thought she would surely be torn in two. Just when she thought herself incapable of containing it any longer, Nick thrust deep inside her—reaching her core in his release and releasing her as well. The tightly wound spring uncurled in a whiplash of molten desire.

Nick pulled her tightly against him. He'd never known a union so strong that he could lose himself to the extent that he didn't know where he ended and she began. The idea that they shared such a powerful bond should have scared the ever-loving daylights out of him, but it didn't.

She chose that moment to snuggle against him, her sighs mingling with his. He looked down at her, soft curves and sleek strength. She matched him perfectly and he knew he'd never again feel this close to another person. *What if it hadn't affected her the same way?* He hated to admit how afraid he was to find out.

As if sensing his inner battle, Willa tilted her head up to look at him. What Nick saw sent a rush of relief shooting through him, followed swiftly by a sense of pride so strong he was almost embarrassed by it. His voice came out in a husky rumble. "Your smile would put the Cheshire cat to shame."

"Yeah, well, you look ready to crow yourself," she responded, her smile provocative, her voice whiskey rough.

Nick placed the pad of his finger against her

lips, stroking their bruised fullness. "I should have been gentler, gone slower the first time."

She shook her head; the way he looked at her made her feel strangely invincible and she wanted him to feel the same. "You said before that my response to you was beautiful because it was honest. Do you know how incredible you made me feel? I have never felt so desirable in my life." She slowly pulled the tip of his finger into her mouth and began to suck on it—amazed and incredibly pleased that there was no awkwardness between them. Her eyes widened when she felt him stir inside her.

"Don't look at me like that," he admonished. "You're the one tempting fate." At her quizzical look he said, "I want you. Don't ever doubt that. It's just that—well, you may not be sore now, but by tomorrow you might wish you'd never laid eyes on me."

Willa's immediate reaction to his teasing assumption was to deny it vigorously. Her fingers dug unconsciously into his shoulders. "Nothing could ever make me regret what we just shared." Nick's muttered expletive startled her, and she belatedly realized how tightly she must have been gripping him. "I'm sorry. Did I hurt you?"

"No, baby, never." He stroked her hair and kissed her gently before easing out of her. "Hurting is having to leave this bed, and you. That's my only regret." When Willa still looked confused, he added, "It's late and we have to get back to the club."

The club! How could she have completely forgotten about her job—not to mention what was in store for her later this evening. She glanced at Nick and found him absorbed in studying the shiny curl he had wrapped around his finger. *You know exactly how it happened.* In that moment she could have blanked out the world if it meant keeping him here with her.

"I'll use the shower in the guest room. You can use the master bath." Nick smiled at her obvious disappointment. "Next time we'll shower together, I promise." He pressed a kiss between her eyebrows and rolled out of bed.

The pain in his knee was intense as the blood rushed through his legs, but it was a small price to pay. He scooped up his scattered clothing and limped to the door.

Next time . . . Willa was completely besotted and couldn't have taken her eyes off Nick's beautifully sculpted body if threatened with death. As he strode to the door she noted with delight the curved sides of his muscled buttocks. He was built like a statue. She dipped her head, suppressing a giggle. This man was definitely not made of stone—just hard as one. *Oh Willa, you've got it bad!*

Nick turned at the door and caught Willa's supremely feminine smile. He flashed a like-what-you-see grin and a sexy wink—totally at ease with his nudity—then ducked out the door to escape the fluffy pillow she heaved at him.

Willa clasped her arms around her knees, wrapped in a sensual fog and unwilling to let it fade. Making love with Nick had far surpassed her wildest expectations. His complete absorption in her had caused that seedling of hope within her to grow, nurtured by the golden light of their lovemaking.

They did have a chance. She knew it.

Sitting on the bed in his guest bedroom, Nick waited for the sound of the shower running in the master bath before dialing the phone. He rubbed his throbbing knee while he punched in Willa's home phone number, his shaky fingers a testament to how affected he still was by what they had shared. He let it ring once and hung up, pausing a moment before dialing the number again. After several rings a masculine voice came on the line. Nick sighed in relief. "Sky, thank God, I was afraid you'd already left."

"I was just about to leave. What took so long?"

Sky was Nick's closest friend, but Nick wasn't ready to tell him about the change in his relationship with Willa. "I guess her key was still under the rock. What did you find?"

"I had to turn over a dozen rocks before I found the damn thing, but it was there. I guess it turned out to be a lucky break that she told me where her spare was hidden after locking herself out one night."

"Yeah, lucky. What did you find?" Nick didn't know how long he could talk safely and hoped Sky would hurry up.

"Well," Sky explained, "this is a big house and Miller could have stashed the drugs in a million places, but I concentrated my search on the first floor."

"And . . . and? Don't keep me in suspense, Sky."

"I took your advice and looked in the same general places that he used in your house. I found four packets."

"Damn!" Nick jammed his fingers through his hair. "I knew it. I should have seen this coming."

"Don't beat yourself up over this. When Eric planted stuff in your house, he did it during your backyard barbecue for the kids. We had no way of knowing he'd be desperate enough to break into Willa's home to set her up."

"I still should've been more aware. I know better than anyone what Miller's capable of." Nick bit off an expletive, careful to keep his voice down, even though he could still hear the shower running. Willa had enough to deal with right now and he'd be damned if Miller would hurt her again. "Did you make the switch?"

"Uh-huh. I'll drop the real stuff off at Boxleitner's office on my way back to the club, and see if he's come up with anything on Doc." Sky was silent for a moment, then said, "Miller's going to a lot of trouble to ensure Willa's cooperation."

"Yeah. You were right about him being desperate. But he's still smart enough to cover his bases. Seeing me at the club with Willa must have shaken him." Nick realized that the stakes were getting dangerously high.

"I've got to be on my way if I'm going to meet Box and get back to the club before my next client." Sky paused, then said quietly, "Are you sure you shouldn't tell her? This is getting dangerous. You know how I feel about all this sneaking around."

Nick thought about that for a long minute.

After what had transpired between them, his protective instincts where Willa was concerned were running pretty high. "No, Sky, I don't think so. At least not now. I know how you feel, and I can't tell you how much I appreciate what you've done for me. Just trust me a while longer, buddy."

Sky heaved a sigh that made his feelings on the matter clear. "This is your show. But when she finds out, don't blame me if she tears your head off for not trusting her."

"I do trust her, dammit!" Nick stopped and blew out a long sigh. More quietly he added, "The less she knows, the easier it will be to keep her safe."

"I know you care about her, Nick, and you want to protect her. Be careful yourself, okay?"

"Thanks, Sky. Let's hope it will be all over tonight. Then I can clear all this up. But not until we nail Miller."

Willa had been back at the club for over six hours and had dealt with at least as many clients, and she was still floating. Yes, the training/rehab program for off-season athletes had gotten off to a very successful start. But that wasn't the reason she had worked through her busy schedule with an unabashed smile plastered on her face.

She wondered if everyone who laid eyes on her could tell of the monumental change that had taken place in Nick's bed. He had said how strongly he felt about that "something" they shared, but she had never dreamed it would be so intense.

She had to force her mind back to the Pisa-like tower of folders heaped on her desk, the unfortunate result of a busy day. Thankfully, after the interlude with Nick, topped by a hectic day, she'd successfully put off thinking about the night. Given the way she was feeling about Nick right now, she was half afraid she'd tear Eric's head off to force a confession out of him.

That idea brought a devilish smile to her face, which is how Nick found her. Resting his cane on her desk, he lowered himself into the chair facing her and smiled back. "Thinking about me, I hope."

"In a roundabout way, you might say." She looked at the man she had fallen in love with. "Actually I was wondering how to face Eric tonight without wringing his neck."

As much as he hated the subterfuge, the vulnerability and fear lying just beneath her lightly spoken words only served to reaffirm his decision not to tell her about the drugs. She definitely didn't need the added pressure. "That's what I came to talk to you about."

"You want me to wring his neck?"

Nick rewarded her with a flash of white teeth. "Sky will be down in a minute, so we can go over the plan again. I just wanted to see how you were holding up."

"Fine, I guess. I know I'll feel better knowing you're right next door." She started as she realized how much truth there was in that statement. Feeling strangely dependent on him and certain she shouldn't be liking it, she added, "But I doubt Eric will try anything I can't—"

"I'm not too sure about that first part," Nick interrupted. "Eric seems pretty interested in picking up where you two left off. Don't forget he needs you again, and the best way to do that is to make you vulnerable to him."

Nick's remarks struck her dead in the middle of her heart. Her foolish actions eight months ago had haunted her day and night since she found out what she had done. Nick didn't have to remind her what Eric's true motives were. She looked up at Nick and saw no trace of care or concern; his face was more a mask of frustration. For the first time since they had left his house, a horribly painful thought penetrated her romantic fog. *He could be still using you, too, Willa. Remember, you hurt him pretty badly.*

Willa's insecurities over her ability to have a mutually satisfying relationship with a man ran pretty deep. Far deeper than one afternoon in bed with Nick—no matter how soul-stirringly beautiful—could resolve. After all, the first man she thought she loved had only been using her. And though what she'd felt for Eric couldn't compare with the deep, unending feelings she had for Nick, she still questioned what Nick saw in her. What could make him desire a woman he had once thought capable of destroying his career?

What, other than revenge?

Once her mind latched onto this agonizing idea, it was as if a runaway train had taken off with her emotions. *Maybe getting me into bed has been his own private reward,* she thought wildly.

Willa tried to stop, tried to put her wild imaginings in the perspective of what had happened between them that day. But with Nick sitting a scant two feet away, and her damnable body responding to him like a moth to a flame, it was next to impossible.

Thankfully Sky chose that moment to come in, saving her from her thoughts and from having to explain her sudden change in mood to Nick.

She avoided looking directly at Nick and said to Sky, "So, are we all set?"

Sky looked at the two of them, evidently sensing the tension between them, and made a scissor motion with his hands that only Nick could see. A glare from his friend erased the smile on Sky's face.

Nick didn't know what in the hell had come over Willa in the last few minutes. One second she'd looked ready to leap across the desk and rip his clothes off, and the next she couldn't—or wouldn't—even make eye contact with him. He turned to Sky. "Were you able to get that recorder from Box?"

"Yeah, I've got it right here." Sky pulled a tiny dictation-style tape recorder out of his pocket and tossed it on Willa's desk.

"Great." Nick faced Willa, staring hard at her as he spoke, willing her to look at him. She always wore her emotions plainly, at least around him, and if only he could see her eyes, he might be able to figure out what had gone wrong. "It's small enough that you should be able to hide it pretty easily. The mike is powerful, so it can be hidden in a partially opened drawer or your purse and still pick up conversation very well."

Nick leaned back in his chair and swore under his breath as Willa looked calmly at him. If he spent the next hundred years with her, he'd never be able to figure her out.

Yet spending the next fifty or hundred years with her was exactly what he wanted. He'd just have to do whatever it took to convince her that everything would work out between them.

"How do you work this thing?" Willa asked.

Sky leaned over the desk and was going over the tiny machine's finer points when the phone buzzed. She reached across the pile of folders, noticing the cane propped against the front of her desk. She flushed as she remembered how she, a trained therapist, hadn't given a thought to Nick's knee injury during their passionate, very physical lovemaking. She quietly cleared her throat before answering the call. "Yes, Kelly, what is it?"

"I received a message from Mr. Miller."

Willa stiffened to keep from shaking. "Yes? What did he say?"

"He said to apologize, but that something important had come up and he was sure you'd understand."

That was the last thing she'd expected to hear. "He canceled?"

A collective groan went up in the room and Willa covered her other ear to hear what Kelly was saying. "He told me to tell you that he would catch up with you later."

The sudden burst of agitated conversation swirling around her made it difficult to hear all of Kelly's explanation. "Did he make another training appointment?"

"No, he didn't. Uh, the club is empty and I've filed the client folders. Is it all right if I leave?"

Willa sighed wearily. "Sure. Check again to make sure the place is cleared out, then lock the front door on your way out." She resisted the urge to slam the receiver back into its cradle, replacing it gently before looking up at the two men. "What now?"

Nick was holding his cane like a matchstick he'd like to snap in two. "I've waited this long, I guess I can wait until he reschedules."

Sky nodded in agreement and turned to Willa. "If you want to get out of here, I can close up for you." It was obvious that he was trying to make it easier for Nick and Willa to leave together.

Willa shook her head. "Thanks anyway, Sky. I could use the extra time to finish up these new files." She didn't add that she was only back-logged because she had spent the better part of the last hour reliving in every delicious detail her time in bed with Nick.

Averting her gaze, certain that Nick was reading her mind, she rearranged a few of the stacks in front of her and said, "You go on, you've been here since the crack of dawn. Besides," she added, smiling her thanks, "you've done more than enough today." Willa was too distracted about being left alone with Nick to question Sky's hurried good-bye and the flush staining his cheeks as he left.

Nick studied Willa for a moment, not at all sure about her current frame of mind. He wasn't sure about his either. Amazingly, his first thought when he heard Miller wasn't coming was an incredible sense of relief that Willa wouldn't have to spend more time alone with him.

For eight long months, to the exclusion of everything else, his whole life had focused on clearing his name and seeing justice done. So how had he fallen so hard, so fast? The way he felt about her, even now that her behavior was a far cry from that of the intoxicatingly beautiful woman who'd moved passionately beneath him only hours ago, matching him thrust for thrust— even now, no longer the satisfied loving partner, but a frightened confused lady—he knew that if she asked him to drop this whole thing, he'd do it.

Willingly.

That was how hard he'd fallen.

Willa was busy trying to generate an interest in her work and didn't hear him rise to rest his hip against her desk. When he spoke, the nearness of his low-timbred rasp left her trembling, her slim thread of control unraveling as fast as her ability to reason had earlier.

"I could stay until you're done."

Her heart was pounding in her throat. She wanted nothing more than to go around her desk and fall into his arms. "No, that's not necessary. I really do have some catching up to do." The words were choked out, barely achieving the controlled tone she fought so hard to maintain. She ruined the effect by blushing furiously, but couldn't seem to stop herself from adding, "I'm sure your knee must be killing you. When is your next session with Richard?"

"Wednesday. Are you sure you don't want me to stay?"

Yes! No! Willa sensed from his tone that it was more than a polite request. She summoned up the strength to look at him—really look at him—for the first time since her doubts about his motivation for taking her into his arms and into his bed had flooded her brain, rendering her incapable of rational thought.

"No, Nick," she lied. "I'll be okay."

His expression changed instantly, as if metal

doors had clanged shut over eyes that, only moments ago, looked as if they could melt steel. She'd never felt so completely alone in her life.

Nick slid off the desk, retrieved his cane, and moved slowly toward the door, giving her plenty of time to call him back. She had to bite down hard on the inside of her cheek to keep from doing just that.

He paused with one hand on the knob. His head dipped as he swore violently and abruptly crossed back to her desk—more quickly than she had believed possible. Moving around her desk, he dropped his cane carelessly to the floor and hauled her up out of her chair. Hands clamped on her shoulders, he slanted his mouth hard across hers. The kiss was short, almost over before it started. But in those few seconds he branded her with all the heat and passion, the pain and confusion he was feeling, leaving her breathless long after he'd gone.

NINE

Willa lost track of how long she stood staring sightlessly at the office door Nick had closed none too gently. When she could move, she moved a trembling fingertip over her lips, amazed at the impact one kiss could have on her entire system. Had she been coherent, she would have begged him to stay and discuss her fears.

If they proved groundless, she risked losing the best thing that had ever happened to her.

But what if she was right, and he *had* been using her? Insidious doubts seemed to have taken up residence in her soul, unconquerable in the face of her past and the confusion of her present. Exhausted, both physically and emotionally, Willa still spent several hours clearing her desk, hoping the task would keep her mind off Nick. It failed miserably.

It was very late when she drove up to her house. The three-quarter moon cast eerie shadows across the stand of oak trees, and she didn't notice the sleek, black sports car in the drive until she almost ran into the back of it.

Despite her vow to put some distance between Nick and herself, her heart gave a crazy lurch. Had he traded in his Texas-sized rental for a smaller, European model? Her heart slowed to an ominous thud as she belatedly recognized the black Porsche. *Eric!*

Unable to see the interior in the moonlight, she cut a wide path around the car. *All this spy stuff is making you paranoid*, she told herself, shivering despite the unseasonable warmth of the night. When no one leaped out of the car, she felt ridiculous and turned toward the house, then screamed as Eric chose that moment to emerge from the shadows of the front porch.

"Willa, is that you?" Eric's voice was annoyingly petulant. "You really should leave a light on out here. I almost killed myself tripping over some loose rocks."

Barely resisting the urge to punch him for scaring her so badly, she snapped, "I hardly think your life was in danger, Eric. As for the lack of light, I hadn't planned on being out late."

"I've been here for almost an hour. Where

have you been?" he demanded peevishly. He didn't add, "With whom," but it was clearly implied in his tone of voice.

"We had an appointment to meet hours ago, which, if you recall, *you* were the one to cancel." Considering the late hour and the isolated area, Willa knew it was foolish to give in to her temper, but she couldn't stop herself. "As for what I was doing, that's none of your damn business."

Eric stepped closer. He was as angry as she, and the look on his face made her take an involuntary step back. Eric's gleaming smile looked sinister in the moonlight, bringing instantly to mind his quicksilver mood changes the night at the restaurant and in the parking lot.

"Oh, but your business will be my business. That's what I came to talk to you about." He stepped forward and gently but firmly grabbed her upper arm and pulled her up onto the porch.

As she fumbled in her bag for her house key, her hand fell on the little recorder that Sky had given her. She ran her fingers over it and pressed what she hoped was the right combination of buttons. Maybe she could turn this unexpected visit to her advantage after all. Armed with a plan of sorts, she mustered a ragged, but serviceable facade of calm.

Eric didn't loosen his grip on her arm as she

entered the house, flipping on every light switch within reach of her free hand. "Eric, why don't you go on into the family room while I get us something to drink. I don't know about you, but it's been a long day and I could use some wine." She spoke in a hurry while tugging her arm free.

Once in the kitchen, she grabbed the phone, pulling the cord to the door so she could keep tabs on Eric. *Come on, Nick, answer,* she pleaded silently. *I need you.*

"Willa? What's taking so long?"

No answer. *Damn.* She hung up, only briefly allowing herself to wonder where Nick could be this late at night. After her rebuff she couldn't help but wonder. . . . *No. I can't think about that now.* She hurried to pour Eric a glass of wine, opting for grape juice for herself and hoping he wouldn't notice the difference. She debated trying to reach Sky, but Eric called her again, forcing her to abandon that idea. She gripped the two glasses and headed for the front room.

"About damn time." Eric's words were more growled than spoken; his mood had shifted again. Willa went to sit in the chair by the fireplace, but Eric patted the seat next to him on the couch. "We have a lot to discuss." His expression challenged her.

Trying to appear as if the very thought of

being close to him didn't nauseate her, she nodded. "Fine, have it your way."

"I always do," he responded, his perfectly capped teeth exposed by his confident grin.

Willa prayed he couldn't see her shiver. Eric was smug almost to the point of arrogance. Gone was any trace of the eager-to-please man trying to curry her favor.

"You said you came to talk to me," she said, determined to take control of the conversation. "So explain what you meant the other day when you said that renewing our relationship would be mutually rewarding." Willa resisted the urge to look at the leather handbag she had dropped on the side table. She couldn't afford to draw his attention to it, she could only pray the recorder was working.

Eric wandered over to the tightly packed bookshelves that framed the stone fireplace, running his hands over the dusty spines. "Yes. As a matter of fact I want to propose a business deal to you. Actually, I'd like to propose a lot more, but I don't have time to play your little games."

Despite her uneasiness he'd piqued her curiosity. The slightly manic look in Eric's eyes was making it difficult for her to concentrate. *I can't do this alone. Nick, where are you?*

Taking a discreet breath to steady her voice,

she said, "No games, Eric. I'm always open to increasing my income. So what is this all about?"

Nick paced back and forth across his living-room floor, having abandoned any attempt at sleep hours before. His cool cotton sheets, scented with Willa's fragrance, had driven him crazy the moment he'd crawled between them.

Why had she pushed him away? he'd asked himself for the millionth time since he'd left her office. He'd gone over it again and again, reliving every nuance of their brief parting kiss. But her instant response had given him little if any insight into her reasons for backing off so abruptly.

He did know one thing for certain—the longer he left her alone, the thicker her protective layer would grow.

He snatched up the phone, then slammed it back down. Dammit, she'd locked herself away in her castle for too long and he'd be damned if he'd let her rebuild defenses he thought they'd very effectively destroyed that afternoon. After grabbing his keys and cane, he headed for his sedan.

As he sped along the highway he felt a sudden sense of panic. Something terrible would happen if he didn't get to Willa immediately. He didn't pause to question the feeling, automatically jamming his foot down harder on the pedal.

The wave of anxiety that had him gripping the wheel blotted out the stab of pain shooting through his knee as he raced the car down the rutted lane to Willa's house. He slowed as he caught sight of her little red car, wondering why she'd parked so far back from her front door.

He shut off the engine and pulled himself out of the car, sighing in relief that the lights were on in the front room. *Well, at least she can't sleep either.* He stood a moment, telling himself his panic attack must have been an acute case of nerves. He lifted his cane out of the car, trying out several opening lines as he headed to the house. "Son of a—" A menacing scowl darkened his features as he noticed the Porsche parked in the shadows of the house. Miller!

To his shame, his first thought was that Willa was really in cahoots with Miller, a very feasible explanation for her earlier behavior and one Nick—unconsciously?—hadn't allowed himself to consider. But the shame died quickly, replaced by pure, unadulterated fury. He crept closer to the house until he had a clear view of Willa and Eric cuddled on the couch.

With no real plan other than getting Miller's

paws off his woman, he stormed up to the front porch. *His woman.* "Damn straight," he muttered under his breath, then paused an inch shy of yanking the door off its hinges.

She was his woman. And he was her man.

She was the woman he had chosen to trust with his heart, one he knew told the truth when she said she'd never willingly hurt him.

Which meant— A sliver of dread climbed his spine. How could he have been that stupid . . . even if only for a moment? Slowly he inched over to the edge of the porch, carefully peeking in the window. They were still talking, sitting close. . . .

Eric was smiling and all but drooling over her, and Willa sat next to him, her brittle smile and tightly pressed knees an indication that her coolness was no more than a front.

He couldn't risk Willa's safety by barging in like the cavalry. He had to come up with a plan. Backing away from the front window and off the porch, he stumbled over some loose rocks.

Using his cane for balance, he reached down and felt along the rocks, swearing silently when the moon picked that moment to hide behind the clouds. He groped under several stones before his fingers contacted the small piece of cold metal. Her key. He moved as quickly as he could around the large rambling farmhouse to the entrance to Willa's kitchen. Once inside, he moved to the doorway leading to the hall. Wasting no time once he'd assured himself his entrance had gone undetected, he picked up the phone and stepped into the pantry. Sky answered after two rings.

"Hey, sorry to wake you, buddy, but it's show time," he whispered, quickly going on to explain the situation. By the time he hung up, the adrenaline was pumping through him faster than it had on Super Bowl Sunday. One way or another, it was all coming out tonight.

He crept down the hall so he could hear their conversation, wishing he could let Willa know he was there to help her, praying that she could hold her own until the time was right for him to take over.

Eric shifted a bit closer to Willa, his thigh almost brushing hers, his smile daring her to draw away. She pressed her shoulders down, making a conscious effort to relax, and hid her trembling hands between clenched knees. She wished Eric would get to the point. His rantings about his unfair treatment by the coaching staff had started to turn into raving paranoia that was as frightening as it was boring.

"I'm a Super Bowl–winning quarterback, Willa. And they think they can just shove me aside because of a minor shoulder injury. Well—"

Willa broke in, determined to reason with him. "Have they actually said they were going to replace you?"

He looked at her in that condescending manner she loathed. "Willa, trust me. I'm a pro, and I know what I hear. But I've got it covered. I don't need the NFL and their big contracts. You and I are going into business."

Willa's jaw dropped, then quickly snapped shut. "What business?"

"Dealing. To a very exclusive clientele, of course. The ones with money to spend. All professional sports have their overachievers who need the type of relaxation I intend to supply. And with your new athletic program bringing in the cream of the crop, we'll be raking it in, in no time." He reached out and ran a hand over her knee, still smiling. "Don't look so shocked. I know you were a little naive when we dated, but you've changed, Willa." He leaned closer as he spoke, the unnatural brightness in his eyes impossible to ignore. "Once you've *tasted* the rewards, you'll agree."

Willa was reeling. This was not the man she dated only a year ago. It couldn't be—it was too frightening to think she could have been so blind. She believed now that he'd been taking drugs back then, but this . . . this was the talk of a crazy man. "You're an addict, aren't you?" she blurted out. It all started to make a gut-twisting kind of sense. "It's not the shoulder injury that's hurting your performance, it's the cocaine. Eric, it's only a matter of time before people find out."

Her words had no effect. His smile never faltered. Just sitting near him made her suddenly feel unclean . . . then another thought hit her. She shot off the couch before he could grab her. "*You* failed the drug test, and set up Nick Logan to take the fall." Her accusation only served to deepen his condescending smile, and Willa lost control. Storming over to him, wanting nothing more than to claw that damn smirk off his face, she demanded, "Why Nick Logan, Eric? And why did you go so far as to have him arrested? Wasn't switching the test results and getting him banned enough for you? What could he possibly have done to deserve that?"

Eric snaked out a hand and yanked her back on the couch. "You really are a little fool. Don't you think I knew they would test the whole team again if I didn't make it believable that Nick Logan, our own 'Mr. Clean,' was a cokehead? Why are you so concerned, anyway? He's only an offensive tackle, Willa, and they're a dime a dozen. I'm the top quarterback in the league!"

Nick shook with barely controlled rage at Eric's callous words. Blood pounded through his veins with such force he couldn't hear himself think. He darted a look around the corner as Eric shoved Willa's arm down and stood up. He would pay for that first, Nick decided, fists clenched, ready for battle. Unless Sky brought the entire force with him, Miller was not going to leave this house without a few serious medical problems.

This had gone on long enough. Nick refused to subject Willa to more. To hell with clearing his name. If the authorities didn't believe his word about Miller, then to hell with them too. He stepped to the doorway, but Willa's voice, cold as steel, stopped him in his tracks.

"You egotistical bastard!" Shaking with fury, she demanded, "How could you ruin a man's life just to save your own miserable neck?"

Eric stopped his pacing and turned on Willa. "You think I don't know what has you so upset? You and Logan are thick as thieves. Did you think I actually bought all that 'let's be friends and talk about the past' crap? Well, Miss High-and-Mighty, you're pretty damned righteous considering you helped me frame him." He stalked over to her, and even as angry as she was, Willa's eyes widened and she sank down onto the chair behind her. "Yes, you! Those were some pretty powerful vitamins you delivered to Doc for me. Came in real handy when I decided to plant them on Nick."

His smile was demonic. "What about Doc? How did you get to him?"

"He was real eager to help me. Thanks for the intro, by the way, I couldn't have done it without him. He thinks the world of you, you know—but he also had some rather large outstanding debts to a few nasty characters that he was more than willing to let me pay off in exchange for switching test results."

Willa sank further into the chair. Nick had been right all along. Eric and Doc had both betrayed her. She couldn't trust anyone, not even herself. A fresh wave of anger surged through her, intensifying as she thought how Nick's life had been forfeited to another man's desperation.

"I think that if you want to save your skin—your very pretty skin—you'll reconsider my earlier offer." Eric reached out and touched her cheek, the contact startling Willa out of her trancelike state of fury.

Jerking away, she asked. "Tell me, Eric, why Nick?"

"Yes," boomed a very deep voice from the doorway. "Why don't you answer the lady."

Both Willa and Eric jumped at the sound of Nick's voice.

"Nick! What are you doing here? Thank Go—"

"Logan," Eric interrupted. He pulled Willa up by her arm, which he kept in a viselike grip. "I should have known you'd show up. You're just in time to join the party. I was explaining to Willa how helpful she can be in our new business endeavor."

Willa struggled against him. "Let me go!" Eric tightened his grip painfully, his smile never faltering. *This is all wrong*, she thought feverishly. *Why isn't Eric nervous?* Nick's expression was implacable. Could he believe she was in league with Eric? Redoubling her struggle, she tugged frantically on her arm. "Nick, it's not what you—"

"Let her go, Miller." There was no mistaking the cold menace in Nick's tone, yet Eric didn't relax his grip.

"I think you've lost again, Logan. Your lady here is going to help me with my new career. As a matter of fact, I'm willing to bet she'll be begging to help me."

"I wouldn't be too sure of that, Miller. Now let her go—or this time when they arrest me, I'll be guilty as hell and the charges will be a whole lot more serious than dealing dope."

Eric's eyes gleamed brighter and Willa swore she heard a snarling sound from Nick. Whether sensing a close brush with death or merely changing tactics, Eric dropped her arm.

"Fine, have it your way." Eric moved casually to the other side of the room. A small contented smile played across his face as he glanced at the bookshelves.

"From now on I intend to." Nick pulled Willa to his side and wrapped his arm around her waist. "You never did answer the lady. Why me? Surely you had a better reason than my supposedly expendable talents?"

Eric laughed and turned to face them. "Actually, Logan, I guess you could say you were born to the wrong parents."

"What in the hell do they have to do with this?"

"Nothing." He chuckled as if vastly amused by his private joke. "You see, I didn't care who it was. I picked the next guy on the list that tested clean. Logan comes right before Miller, so by virtue of your last name, you won."

Willa tore out of Nick's grasp and stormed across the room. Jabbing a finger in Eric's chest, she said, "You mean to tell me that you wasted a man's career and his life because he was the most *convenient* alphabetically?"

In a soft voice filled with menace, Nick said, "Willa, come back here. I appreciate your defense, but I want to handle this." Willa grudgingly seated herself on the couch, out of harm's way, and Nick turned to Miller. "You smug, arrogant son of a bitch. What in the hell were you going to do the next year? Doc's retired. Willa's onto your game. How is a dopehead like you going to pass the next test? Assuming they don't drop you first."

Eric smiled as if Nick was a little slow on the uptake. "That's just it, Logan. There won't be a next time. I don't need the NFL or those back-stabbing coaches. So I like to snort a little to help me relax, it doesn't make me an addict. Besides, that's not why I'm retiring."

"Retiring?" Willa and Nick spoke as one.

"Surprised? You shouldn't be. When are you going to realize that I'm one step ahead of all of you? I figure the networks can't wait to offer me a nice cushy commentary job. Between that and my little sideline with Willa, I'll be set. I'll go out on top. Why risk this pretty face for another season of being a tackling dummy?"

"You're more messed up than I thought if you

still think I'm going into any business with you—legal or not."

Eric seemed very pleased by her outburst. Chuckling, he turned back to the bookshelf, pulling out one of the less dusty volumes. A small white packet slid neatly into his palm. He dangled it between his fingers like a hypnotizing pendant. "This is why, my dear. I doubt the manager of one of the country's finest training facilities is going to risk having the media find out about her sizable drug habit."

Willa was mute with surprise. Eric turned his condescending grin on Nick. "And as far as relating this evening's discussions to the media, I wouldn't advise it. It will be your word against mine, and we all know how much your word is worth these days." He walked over to the table, dropping the packet on it before sitting on the couch and patting the place next to him as he had earlier. "Now be a good girl, Willa, and tell Mr. Logan to leave. We have business to discuss."

Nick glanced away from the window, apparently the only one to notice the trail of headlights parading down Willa's drive. He returned Eric's smile, looking every bit as confident. "I guess we'll find out who believes what real soon."

Willa swung her gaze back and forth between the two men. Her head was still spinning from

Eric's threats and she couldn't comprehend why they were both strutting around like playground braggarts instead of beating the living hell out of each other. Then she remembered.

Leaping up, she quickly ran across the room, grabbing her purse off the table, frantically digging in it to no avail until she forced herself to calm down. Taking a deep breath to steady her nerves, she finally located the cool metal recorder. *Please God, let it be working.*

It was! She shouted in delight and swung around to tell Nick when the front door burst open and Sky strolled in followed by the largest black man Willa had ever seen. It wasn't until the giant moved into the room that she noticed there were several policemen behind him.

In a deep rumbling bass the giant said, "Hello, folks, I'm Detective Frank Boxleitner." He flipped open his wallet. "DEA. And these gentlemen"—he gestured to the men behind him—"are from the sheriff's department."

Before the detective could continue, Eric leaped off the couch and moved to his side. "Hello, sir," he gushed, reaching to shake his hand. "Thank God you've come." He swung an accusing finger at Nick and Willa. "These two people have brought me here under false pretenses. This is Nick Logan and Willa Trask.

They were trying to sell me drugs." He ran to the table and scooped up the packet, almost flinging it at the large man. "See? I'm sure you remember Mr. Logan from his recent drug trial. Well, I'm sure glad you arrived when you did."

Willa was trying to figure out why Nick wasn't heatedly denying Eric's story when he strolled to the mantel and lifted the old clock, peeling a packet off the bottom. Eric's face went deathly pale.

"Box, nice to see you again. Here." Nick tossed the packet to him. "I think if you'll taste this, you'll find that the only thing Miss Trask has stashed is sugar."

Eric snatched the bag out of the air, his face contorted in anger as he realized he'd been had. Willa dazedly tried to put everything that had happened into some kind of order. Clenching her hands in frustration, she remembered the recorder. She gave it to the large detective. "Detective, I think if you'll listen to this, it'll explain everything."

Willa turned to Nick with a triumphant smile, fully expecting he'd drag her back into his arms and reward her with kisses of approval and admiration. Instead she encountered a sudden fierceness, then in the next second he was launching himself at her. It was only because she ducked instinctively that Eric's desperate lunge for her came up short. A split second later he was smashed to the floor with a loud thump as Nick hit the target of his flying tackle.

The police had been a little slow to respond to the sudden burst of action, but now they hurried to pull Nick off Eric, only releasing him when he promised to calm down.

He immediately hobbled over to Willa, cupping her cheek. "You okay? I couldn't warn you, but you have great instincts, you know. Must be in the genes." He pressed a hard kiss on her lips, so relieved she was okay that he misread her stiff posture as shock over nearly being tackled. He thought about kicking everyone out and taking her upstairs, but Sky tapped his shoulder and he reluctantly lifted his head.

"Box'd like to talk to each of you separately if you're ready to give your statements. They've previewed enough of the tape to warrant taking Miller in for questioning." Grinning broadly, Sky hauled Nick into a tight bear hug. "We did it, man. We nailed the bastard."

Nick responded with a fierce hug of his own, then stumbled slightly when Sky released him. He immediately doubled over and grabbed his knee.

Willa responded immediately to his groan of

pain. She knelt and probed around his knee, then gently pushed him into a sitting position on the floor.

He looked up into her worry-filled eyes, a cocky smile creasing his face. "Thanks, Princess." He pulled her head close and kissed her again, briefly but thoroughly. "You did it. You saved me. Now let me up so I can tell these guys what they need to know. I want to talk to you and we're wasting time."

Willa fought hard, barely resisting the temptation to touch Nick, to run her hands all over his body, reassure herself that things would be all right. But the nagging suspicion that things weren't what they seemed was too overwhelming to ignore. Thinking was impossible, so she fell back on her professional training and focused all her thoughts on Nick's reinjured knee.

Looking up, she said, "Sky, can you go in the kitchen and get some ice?" When Nick started to rise, she pushed him back down with one hand without turning. "We need to put something on this before it swells to the size of a grapefruit."

"Don't move, Nick. You can talk to the police later."

And then you can answer a few questions of mine, she added silently. *Like how did you know about the phony drugs planted in my house and why in the hell were you conveniently here when Miller showed up?* As if floodgates had opened, one inconsistency after another rushed into her mind. She jumped when a policeman tapped her shoulder.

"They're ready for you now, Miss Trask." His tone was polite but firm. She needed some time and space and quashed the desire to have it out with Nick here and now. Besides, she was too strung out to mount any kind of interrogation and she was too damned scared that she already knew what his answers would be.

Sky had already gathered ice and towels, and with events happening so quickly she didn't stop to wonder how he'd known where to find everything. "Make sure he stays here until his knee is well iced, Sky. Get your detective friend to sit on him if necessary." Sky nodded and with supreme effort she avoided Nick's heated gaze and followed the officer into the dining room.

TEN

It was almost daylight before Willa finally tumbled, completely exhausted, into bed. Her questioning had lasted a long time, during which Sky had convinced Nick he needed to go to the hospital to have his knee examined. They were leaving just as she stepped back into the front room. Nick had refused to let her accompany him, insisting that she rest. She'd barely managed to remove her clothes and pull down the sheets before falling into a thankfully dreamless sleep.

Now it was late afternoon and she still felt exhausted. After a long shower she dragged herself downstairs and fixed a cup of coffee. She had the presence of mind to call the club's CEO and explain that she needed a temporary leave of absence. She must have sounded as bad as she felt, because he gave in without too much hassle. She went back to her bedroom.

Despite the warm spring sun shining through the window, Willa tucked her down comforter around her and slowly sipped her coffee while relentlessly forcing her mind over and over each excruciating detail of the preceding several days.

No matter how she looked at last night's events, Nick still had to have set it up, using her as bait without telling her. Had their whole relationship been a charade? The full range of that possibility had become increasingly, unavoidably, and most painfully clear as she'd tried to reconstruct what had happened for the police. She went over it again and again and she still couldn't find a plausible, painless explanation for everything.

After another hour of hashing it out with herself all over again, her fatigued system simply refused to let her think about it anymore. Yawning widely, she gave up. After switching off her phone, she dropped off into a sound sleep.

By Thursday morning the news of Eric's arrest was splashed over every newspaper in the country. The phone rang incessantly with reporters begging for interviews, but years of experience during her father's illness had taught Willa how to handle them. And she put up with it mainly because she was reluctant to unplug the phone in case Nick or Sky called. But they didn't. Even when she'd swallowed her pride and placed a few calls herself, she'd been unsuccessful in reaching either of them.

Looking out her bedroom window, Willa finally accepted the devastating truth. Eric had been arrested, as had Doc Abbott—another devastating blow—and if the media could be believed, it was a foregone conclusion that they would be convicted. So except for her testimony at their trials, her usefulness to Nick had ended in the early hours of Tuesday morning.

When the yawning ache in her chest threatened to open up and consume her, she turned to the only defense strong enough to get her through the next minute, and the next one, until she could find some way to survive: anger.

Turning away from her bedroom window, she threw the empty suitcase in her hand onto her bed, then started methodically emptying her drawers into it. She'd decided just that morning that she wouldn't call Nick or try to reach him again. She'd also decided to get out of town for a few days—to escape the press, she told herself.

She angrily wiped the tears that had started

coursing down her face. "Don't you dare cry for him, Willa Trask!" Going to the armoire, she swept the jumbled contents into her arms and threw them into a second case she'd dropped on the floor earlier. *You knew this was going to happen,* she lectured herself sternly, *so you have no right to feel sorry for yourself.*

On her way to her car she paused by her answering machine, her eyes misting again as she pulled her hand back from activating it, reaching instead to yank the cord out of the wall. The last thing she needed when she returned was to wade through endless messages in the vain hope that Nick would have called to beg forgiveness. The deafening silence of the last two days had been enough. She peered out the front window to make sure there were no more reporters lurking about.

Throwing her bags in the back of her car, she spun gravel as she headed down her driveway. She'd decided to take a couple of her father's old friends out in Middleburg up on a standing offer to stay at their bed-and-breakfast. The state district attorney had asked that she remain accessible during the trial preliminaries, so she'd alerted him regarding her plans, adding a polite request that he not tell *anyone* where she was.

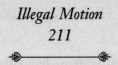

Nick drove down the rutted lane to Willa's house, breaking every last one of his doctor's orders about resting after knee surgery. His knee felt like someone was poking hot daggers into it, but the pain was nothing compared with the ache in his heart when Willa failed to answer the door. He banged a crutch against it and swore. He'd told Sky this would happen.

Damn the doctors and those incompetent nurses for not telling Willa he was in the hospital when she'd called. He'd told himself over and over that that could be the only reason he'd awakened from surgery to peer up at Sky's hulking frame bending over him, instead of opening his eyes to her beautiful face.

While Nick had been in the operating room Sky had tried, unsuccessfully, to get the hospital administrator to change his position on not releasing Nick's identity. The media circus that had resulted from Eric's arrest and Nick's redemption had made every hospital in the area prime hunting ground for the gaggle of snooping reporters who had ferreted out the information that Nick had reinjured his knee during the melee and were looking to get the scoop on an exclusive.

Still groggy from surgery, he'd tried to call

her Tuesday afternoon, but either she wasn't answering or her machine was broken. Sky had tried again and again on Wednesday, but had been unable to get through. When they questioned Box, he said she'd been in Wednesday morning to give her statement. Sky offered to go hunt her down, but by then Nick had begun to sense that something was terribly wrong and knew he had to see her face-to-face.

He demanded to be released as soon as they could do the paperwork, but his doctor had refused even to consider it until Thursday morning. Had it not been for Sky's threats, he would have gotten up and hobbled out of there, release or not. He couldn't fight the notion that every second he wasted in not finding her was one more second she'd have to run away from him forever. And he wouldn't let that happen.

Nick eased his aching frame down until he was sitting on Willa's front porch. He absently noticed how the bulbs in the flower bed under the window had been trampled as if someone had been standing on them trying to get a look into the house. He briefly thought about doing the same thing, but looking up, he saw that the drapes had been tightly drawn. He hadn't even known the front window had drapes.

"Damn," he swore loudly, swatting at his leg, then cursed a blue streak as the pain made him see stars. Because he'd been shielded from them, it hadn't occurred to him until that moment that she'd be a focus of the media's attention too.

He had to find her. He already knew that she'd taken a leave of absence from work. He thought she'd done the right thing, but apparently she'd felt the need to get away from everyone . . . including him.

He levered himself up and went to his car. He drove—more slowly this time—back out to the highway. One way or another he'd find her. And when he did, he wouldn't leave her until she'd agreed to be his forever.

It had been three weeks since Eric's early-morning arrest. His trial wasn't scheduled for another month. Willa almost hoped it would be delayed. "You're going to have to face him sooner or later," she murmured to the empty room. Saying it out loud didn't make it easier to accept. She'd successfully eluded the press, but escaping the memory of Nick Logan had proved impossible. She couldn't stop thinking about him—or stop loving him.

She didn't have much pride left where Nick

Logan was concerned, and she was afraid she'd lose what was left when she saw him again. The trial loomed on the horizon and she could only hope that the impersonal nature of a courtroom would help her maintain her composure.

After that, she would never have to face him again.

She sat at the table, tears streaming down her face, damning herself for not being able to stop loving him. Her mind kept traveling back to that wonderful time spent with Nick in his large mahogany bed. The soaring highs he'd taken her to, the tender words and teasing laughter they'd shared. She had replayed it in her mind so many times, she was sure she had idealized it beyond reality. In a way it was both a salvation and a curse.

She let her mind drift away yet again, then decided she needed to stop once and for all when she heard what sounded like a medieval rendition of the theme from *Rocky*. "Now you've gone completely around the bend. You've even added music."

Realizing the sounds were coming from outside, curiosity drew her to the front door. She blinked, rubbed her eyes, and blinked again. Standing, or rather prancing, looking larger than life in the postage-stamp-size front yard, was a magnificent white stallion. Astride the humongous beast, his black hair whipping in the spring breeze, was Nick. He was wearing western boots, faded jeans with worn knees, and if she wasn't hallucinating—an armored breastplate. He wielded a very large shiny shield in one hand, and the music, which she realized now was a royal fanfare, blared from the boombox balanced on the saddle horn in front of him.

He was an incredibly potent mixture of modern-day cowboy and medieval warrior. He was her knight in armor.

Hands trembling, she opened the front door, but remained standing on the threshold, unwilling to be the first to speak.

"I understand there is a damsel here in serious distress." Nick's deep, powerful voice reverberated across the tiny yard. "I am here to relieve her of all doubts, fight to the death if necessary, to prove her knight's steadfastness."

Fresh tears glittered on her lashes. Drawn by the sheer force of him, she slowly walked out onto the porch. Shielding her eyes from the glare of the sun, she looked up at him; the fierce look of desire and yearning blazing from his eyes immobilized her.

Without taking his eyes from her, Nick leaned over to drop the shield and boombox to the ground. Neither noticed the clang of noise or the music that wobbled to a halt. Next came the breastplate. It crashed to the ground, leaving him bare-chested and strangely vulnerable to her, even from his lofty perch.

After Sky had intercepted her call to the club earlier that day, he'd told Nick she'd been distant, her voice flat and unemotional. Sky's theory was that Willa was still dealing with the hurt she'd experienced in seeing Eric's true nature revealed, followed by the painful betrayal of Doc Abbott.

But the mere fact that in the few minutes she'd spoken to Sky she'd never voiced any interest in Nick or his well-being fairly shouted at Nick her frame of mind. It had taken fifteen minutes of sweet-talking and cajoling to come up with the address belonging to the phone she'd called from.

"Willa." He spoke quietly. "I know I'm no knight. I told you once that I wasn't a hero. But I sure as hell wanted to be one for you. Tell me where I went wrong."

Emotions warred inside her, part of her angry that he couldn't imagine what her problem might be. But his stated intentions along with the honest confusion she heard in his softly spoken request sent her heart soaring.

Yet she stood her ground, gripping the railing to keep from doing something foolish like flinging herself across the yard into his arms. "There *are* a few things I would like to know."

"Ask me anything."

Willa looked away for a moment, shaken at the intense emotion he'd packed into those three words. The effect of Eric's duplicity had been like a bubble of innocence bursting, Doc's betrayal had been a pain of a different kind, even Sky's loyalty to Nick had hurt, though she understood it. But Nick's ultimate distrust of her after what they'd shared—that had been the crushing blow. "Why didn't you tell me? About the drugs?"

Nick looked confused for a moment. "Didn't Sky explain that when you talked to him? He told me he ex—"

"He told me some of it, but said it was really up to you."

Nick swore softly, her defiant tone and defensive posture announcing that he was dealing with the unapproachable Willa. "Thanks, pal," he muttered. "Some friend you are."

"Oh, I'd say he's a very good friend," Willa retorted. "He broke into my house for you and lurked around the club for months for you. You couldn't buy that kind of loyalty."

Nick winced at her sarcastic tone. She thought he still didn't trust her! As the full implications of that sank in he felt the first twinge of panic. She was feeling betrayed by him, something he'd sworn he'd never do to her. "If it's any consolation, Sky wanted me to tell you right from the start."

"It's not his trust that's important to me."

"Princess, I trust you. Hell, I trusted you with my life. More importantly, I trusted you with my heart. Willa, I love you."

Tears started to trickle down her cheeks and she moved to the stairs. She wanted to believe him so badly that it was a physical ache in her heart.

"Willa, I never meant to hurt you. I'll try to explain why I did what I did, but I need to ask you something first."

"Go ahead."

The first hint of Nick's heart-stopping smile stole across his lips. "Would you happen to have a stepladder?"

She blinked, certain she had heard him wrong. "Stepladder?" When he nodded, his expression grave, she asked, "What the devil for?"

"Because when I hauled myself up on this beast, I didn't plan ahead, and getting down with a bum knee is a bit tricky. And if I don't touch you, kiss you, very soon, I may have to risk surgery again and leap off this damn nag."

Willa swiped at her cheeks, unable to keep

her mouth from twitching. She gave up and laughed out loud.

"That does it," Nick stated, and hauled his leg over the saddle to dismount.

Seeing what he was about to do, Willa rushed down the steps to help him, but got caught up in the tangle of legs and stirrups. They both went crashing to the ground.

Somehow Willa landed on top of Nick. She dragged her hair out of his face, to discover Nick was lying very still beneath her, his lashes thick on his cheeks.

"Nick." She put her hands on either side of his face, peering closely at his closed eyes. "Are you all right?"

He opened one eye and said in a sexy drawl, "I will be as soon as you kiss me. After all, it isn't every day that you have a man literally fall at your feet."

Willa smiled, unable to resist the teasing grin she'd missed for weeks, but made one demand before granting his wish. "Look at me when we kiss?" He immediately opened his eyes. She drew a shaky breath at the desire she saw in their smoky depths.

Nick lifted his hand to the nape of her neck, sliding his large palm beneath her tangled hair, guiding her lips to his, his kiss tender and seeking.

Willa let him probe her lips and drop kisses on her chin and ears before responding and becoming an equal partner.

Nick pulled back slightly and whispered hoarsely against her cheek, "As much as I'd like to make sweet love to you like I have dreamed about every night for weeks, I want everything cleared up first."

Nick waited in the small sitting room while Willa made coffee, glad for the chance to get his raging libido under some semblance of control. He glanced at the stairs that led to the upper rooms, unable to keep from picturing Willa's body arching up to accept him, sinking into her, being possessed by her again. . . . Nick shifted uncomfortably. Being noble had its downside.

Willa entered with two steaming mugs of coffee and Nick was relieved when she sat down next to him, though not as close as he would have liked.

Willa spoke first, her words tumbling out in a rush. "If you didn't want to hurt me, then why didn't you tell me about the cocaine? Didn't you think I had a right to know?"

Nick winced. "At first it was because I didn't know how you'd react. After that scene in the parking lot, I . . . I wanted to protect you. You had enough just dealing with Miller, and I didn't think you needed the added pressure of knowing just how devious he was. I thought . . . hell, I guess I wasn't thinking. I told you, I'm new to this knight business. I trust you, Willa, and I know you don't want anyone taking care of you—but dammit, I can't seem to stop wanting to try." Willa's tremulous smile encouraged him. "And please don't be mad at Sky. He didn't like all of it, but he wasn't just being loyal to me, he wanted to protect you too."

"He already apologized." She paused, dipping her head before saying softly, "Nick, I owe you an apology . . . about Doc."

Nick pulled her into his arms at the pain that flickered in the depths of her eyes at the mention of her old friend. "I'm so sorry I wasn't there with you through all that."

She didn't pull away from his embrace, allowing herself finally to draw the strength from him she'd needed for so long. "I saw him on my way here. He's addicted to gambling, Nick. He didn't know what to do, he'd gotten in so far over his head. Eric's offer seemed like a godsend to him."

Nick rubbed her back and lightly traced a finger down her arm. "It's hard for me to be forgiving, I hate what he did to you. I'm sorry, baby, I know he was like family."

"I've lost all respect for him, but I can't hate him. Part of me will always love him for what he once was to me."

Nick gently tipped up her chin. "And what about me?"

Willa's voice trembled, she wanted so badly to erase the uncertainty she saw in his eyes. He really did love her!

"Nick, I—" Her voice broke, but she had to ask. "That afternoon, in your house, when Sky was searching mine . . ."

"My God," Nick whispered. He pulled her around to face him. "Is that what you've been thinking all this time? Do you really think so little of me?"

"Nick, I'm sorry if that hurt. But look at it from my point of view. Everyone I loved, or thought I loved, either lied to me or used me for some self-serving purpose. You had better reason than most, given what you suspected. Then, after the arrest, you didn't need me. You never called me. I couldn't find you. Or Sky. I didn't know what to think."

Nick heaved a huge sigh, wishing now he hadn't been so stubborn about wanting to find her himself and had let Sky track her down immediately. It would have saved them both so much heartache. "Willa, listen to me, because I'm only going to say this once. That day was"—he looked at the ceiling for a moment—"mind-blowing, life changing, more than that. But I certainly didn't need to take you to bed to keep you out of your house for a few hours."

"Nick—" She didn't get a chance to finish. Nick pulled her to him and kissed her with a ferocity that would have been frightening had she not felt the exact same way. She responded fully, with her heart and her soul.

When he pulled away, they were both breathing hard. "The night Eric was arrested, I had no idea he was there. I was coming to see you because I couldn't sleep in my bed—*our* bed—without you. I was coming to tell you that I loved you. Even finding you with Miller didn't stop me from trusting you. If you'd stuck around instead of running, you'd have known that weeks ago."

Willa lightly touched his face, tracing over every line and crease. "I love you, Nick Logan, even when I thought I was being a world-class fool, I couldn't stop loving you."

Nick kissed her again. Happiness stole through him. Their noses touching, he said, "My ban has been lifted and I'm back in everyone's good graces again. Eight months ago that's all I wanted. Right now that means nothing if I don't have your trust."

Willa's eyes sparkled as she flashed him a dazzling grin. "I trust you, Nick. I'll never doubt it again."

Nick trapped her head between his hands, brushing his nose across hers. "Ah, Princess, I love you, but if I don't get your delectable little trusting body upstairs very shortly, we may shock a few of the guests with a very public display of affection."

"There are no guests. Except you." When Nick wiggled his brows, she added, "The owners are friends, but they're out of town at a wedding. So it's just you and me."

"Any more questions?" She shook her head. "Good, because your ten minutes are up."

He scooped her up and headed for the stairs. Willa struggled briefly. "Nick, your knee . . ."

"You're right. I couldn't have waited that long anyway." He placed her gently back on the couch and slowly started to unbutton her blouse. "We'll have plenty of time later to explore the upper realms of your present castle."

Several hours later all was well in Willa's castle. She snuggled next to the hard-muscled length of Nick's warm body. She was drifting off to sleep, thinking that she hadn't embellished on reality one bit—in fact, her memory hadn't done him justice—when Nick nuzzled her awake by pressing light kisses to her hair.

"I wonder if the horse is still there."

"Oh my goodness! I completely forgot." She started to get up, but Nick tightened his hold on her, and she snuggled back down with little resistance. None, actually. "Where did you get the horse and that armor anyway?"

"You'd be amazed what you can rent these days." His voice was still husky from their strenuous afternoon. He was idly twirling her hair around his finger, thinking he was the luckiest man alive. "Don't worry, I'm sure he's fine."

"It must have cost you a fortune."

"Is that a polite way of asking how I'm going to support you?"

"I don't need supporting," was her indignant reply. "I know I've taken a leave of absence, but even if I lose my job, I'm sure I can get another one. My training center will just take a little longer to achieve, that's all."

"Well, I won't have my wife worrying her pretty, not to mention very educated, little head over finances."

Willa smacked him playfully. "Is that your way of asking me to marry you?"

"Well, I'd get down on bended knee, but then I'd have to wait. I can't wait, Willa." He pulled her hard against his body. "I want to spend the rest of my life getting to know everything about you. Will you be my wife?"

"I love you, Nick Logan. I'd be honored."

Nick rolled over and drew her on top of him, dropping kisses onto her shoulder. Willa wriggled on top of him and he groaned, pushing her away a bit.

Willa stilled. "Did I hurt you? Oh, your knee!"

Nick chuckled. "My surgeon's probably out right now putting a down payment on a small island." When Willa started to get up, he tightened his grip. "It hurts, but that's not why I groaned. I just wanted to talk to you before we, uh . . ."

Willa grinned devilishly. "Well, you'd better talk fast."

"While I was trying to find you I did a lot of thinking about our future." Willa raised an eyebrow, but Nick gave her a cocky grin. "My knee is shot, so football is out." He placed a finger across her lips. "It's okay, Willa. Besides, I'm thinking of investing all that money I earned letting people pummel my body in a new venture. What would you think about turning your farm into the training facility you've been wanting to start? We can live at my place—correction, our place."

Willa was dazed by his offer. "Nick, that's wonderful! But it will take up a lot of time. It's a big project."

"Well, I'm not so generous that I'm willing to give my time with you away. You make all the decisions about how the place should be set up. I have only two wishes."

"Anything, sire."

"Oooh, sire, I could get to like that—ouch! Just kidding."

"You better ask quick, buster."

Nick heaved a mock sigh. "Not even married yet and I've already been ousted from my throne." He raised her chin with his finger and kissed her long and hard. "I want to work with you. Got any use for a beat-up ex-jock?"

"Several come to mind." She gave him a sassy wink, then added, "I'd like nothing better than for this to be a team effort all the way."

"Team efforts happen to be my specialty." He pressed his aroused body against her in case she didn't fully comprehend his meaning.

She gasped in helpless desire, but managed to push at his chest. "You said two things, what's the other?"

"I want to save a week or two each summer for the kids to use the facilities. Maybe we can get some of the other pros, both active and retired, to lend their support."

"Nick Logan, have I told you in the last two minutes how much I love you?"

"No. But does that mean yes?"

Willa nodded and Nick's blue eyes turned dark and passionate and he pulled her to him.

"Wait a minute, it's my turn. I have a wish of my own. Remember at your house that day when you mentioned something about showering together?"

Nick's smile turned downright wicked, but he didn't answer. He just got out of bed and disappeared into the bathroom, emerging several long minutes later. In a swirl of jasmine-scented steam, he stood next to the bed. Leaning on his cane, he gave a formal bow and drew Willa's hand into his. "Princess, your bath awaits."

She accepted and they strolled naked into the fog, hands held in the formal court fashion of centuries ago. Their laughter quickly faded into moans of delight, while outside, a very large white horse munched on the hedges.

THE EDITOR'S CORNER

The bounty of six LOVESWEPTs coming your way next month is sure to put you in the right mood for the holiday season. Emotional and exciting, sensuous and scintillating, these tales of love and romance guarantee hours of unbeatable reading pleasure. So indulge yourself—there's no better way to start the celebration!

Leading our lineup is Charlotte Hughes with **KISSED BY A ROGUE**, LOVESWEPT #654—and a rogue is exactly what Cord Buford is. With a smile that promises wicked pleasures, he's used to getting what he wants, so when the beautiful new physician in town insists she won't go out with him, he takes it as a very personal challenge. He'll do anything to feel Billie Foster's soft hands on him, even dare her to give him a physical. Billie's struggle to resist Cord's dangerous temptations is useless, but when their investigation into a mystery at his family's textile mill erupts into steamy kisses under moonlit skies, she has to wonder if she's the one woman who can tame his wild heart. Charlotte's talent shines brightly in this delicious romance.

New author Debra Dixon makes an outstanding debut in LOVESWEPT with **TALL, DARK, AND LONESOME**, #655. Trail boss Zach Weston is definitely all of those things, as Niki Devlin soon discovers when she joins his vacation cattle drive. The columnist starts out interested only in getting a story, but from the moment Zach pulls her out of the mud and into his arms, she wants to scorch his iron control and play with the fire in his gray eyes. However, she believes the scandal that haunts her past can destroy his dreams of happily-ever-after—until Zach dares her to stop running and be lassoed by his love. Talented Debra combines emotional intensity and humor to make **TALL, DARK, AND LONESOME** a winner. You're sure to look forward to more from this New Face of 1993!

Do you remember Jenny Love-Townsend, the heroine's daughter in Peggy Webb's **TOUCHED BY ANGELS**? She returns in **A PRINCE FOR JENNY**, LOVESWEPT #656, but now she's all grown up, a fragile artist who finally meets the man of her dreams. Daniel Sullivan is everything she's ever wished for and the one thing she's sure she can't have. Daniel agrees that the spellbinding emotion between them can't last. He doesn't consider himself to be as noble, strong, and powerful as Jenny sketched him, and though he wants to taste her magic, his desire for this special woman can put her in danger. Peggy will have you crying and cheering as these two people find the courage to believe in the power of love.

What an apt title **FEVER** is for Joan J. Domning's new LOVESWEPT #657, for the temperature does nothing but rise when Alec Golightly and Bunny Fletcher meet. He's a corporate executive who wears a Hawaiian shirt and a pirate's grin—not at all what she expects when she goes to Portland to help bail out his company. Her plan is to get the job done, then quickly return to the fast track, but she suddenly finds herself wildly tempted to run into his arms and stay there. A family is one thing she's never had time for in her race to be the best, but with Alec tantalizing her with his long, slow kisses, she's ready to seize the happiness that has always eluded her. Joan delivers a sexy romance that burns white-hot with desire.

Please welcome Jackie Reeser and her very first novel, **THE LADY CASTS HER LURES**, LOVESWEPT #658. Jackie's a veteran journalist, and she has given her heroine, Pat Langston, the same occupation—and a vexing assignment: to accompany champion Brian Culler on the final round of a fishing contest. He's always found reporters annoying, but one look at Pat and he quickly welcomes the delectable distraction, baiting her with charm that could reel any woman in. The spirited single mom isn't interested in a lady's man who'd never settle down, though. But Brian knows all about being patient and pursues her with seductive humor, willing to wait for the prize of her passion. This delightful romance, told with plenty of verve and sensuality, will show you why we're so excited to be publishing Jackie in LOVESWEPT.

Diane Pershing rounds out the lineup in a very big way with **HEARTQUAKE**, LOVESWEPT #659. A golden-haired geologist, David Franklin prowls the earth in search of the secrets that make it tremble, but he's never felt a tremor as strong as the one that shakes his very soul when he meets Bella Stein. A distant relative, she's surprised by his arrival on her doorstep—and shocked by the restless longing he awakens in her. His wildfire caresses make the beautiful widow respond to him with shameless abandon. Then she discovers the pain he's hidden from everyone, and only her tenderness can heal him and show him that he's worthy of her gift of enduring love. . . . Diane's evocative writing makes this romance stand out.

Happy reading,

With warmest wishes,

Nita Taublib

Nita Taublib

Associate Publisher

P.S. Don't miss the spectacular women's novels Bantam has coming in December: **ADAM'S FALL** by Sandra Brown, a classic romance soon to be available in hardcover; **NOTORIOUS** by Patricia Potter, in which the rivalry and passion between two saloon owners becomes the rage of San Francisco; **PRINCESS OF THIEVES** by Katherine O'Neal, featuring a delightfully wicked con woman and a rugged, ruthless bounty hunter; and **CAPTURE THE NIGHT** by Geralyn Dawson, the latest Once Upon a Time romance with "Beauty and the Beast" at its heart. We'll be giving you a sneak peak at these terrific books in next month's LOVESWEPTs. And immediately following this page, look for a preview of the exciting women's fiction from Bantam *available now!*

Don't miss these exciting books by your favorite Bantam authors

On sale in October:
OUTLAW
by Susan Johnson

MOONLIGHT, MADNESS, & MAGIC
by Suzanne Forster, Charlotte Hughes, and Olivia Rupprecht

SATIN AND STEELE
by Fayrene Preston

And in hardcover from Doubleday
SOMETHING BORROWED, SOMETHING BLUE
by Jillian Karr

Susan Johnson

Nationally bestselling author of
SINFUL and **SILVER FLAME**

Outlaw

*Susan Johnson's most passionate and richly textured
romance yet,* OUTLAW *is the sizzling story of a fierce
Scottish border lord who abducts his sworn enemy, a
beautiful English woman—only to find himself a captive
of her love.*

"Come sit by me then." Elizabeth gently patted
the rough bark beside her as if coaxing a small child
to an unpleasant task.

He should leave, Johnnie thought. He shouldn't
have ridden after her, he shouldn't be panting like
a dog in heat for any woman . . . particularly for
this woman, the daughter of Harold Godfrey, his
lifelong enemy.

"Are you afraid of me?" She'd stopped running
now from her desire. It was an enormous leap of
faith, a rash and venturesome sensation for a woman who'd always viewed the world with caution.

"I'm not afraid of anything," Johnnie answered,
unhesitating confidence in his deep voice.

"I didn't think so," she replied. Dressed like a reiver in leather breeches, high boots, a shirt open at the throat, his hunting plaid the muted color of autumn foliage, he looked not only unafraid but menacing. The danger and attraction of scandalous sin, she thought—all dark arrogant masculinity. "My guardsmen will wait indefinitely," she said very, very quietly, thinking with an arrogance of her own, *There. That should move him.*

And when he took that first step, she smiled a tantalizing female smile, artless and instinctive.

"You please me," she said, gazing up at him as he slowly drew near.

"*You* drive me mad," Johnnie said, sitting down on the fallen tree, resting his arms on his knees and contemplating the dusty toes of his boots.

"And you don't like the feeling."

"I dislike it intensely," he retorted, chafing resentment plain in his voice.

He wouldn't look at her. "Would you rather I leave?"

His head swiveled toward her then, a cynical gleam in his blue eyes. "Of course not."

"Hmmm," Elizabeth murmured, pursing her lips, clasping her hands together and studying her yellow kidskin slippers. "This *is* awkward," she said after a moment, amusement in her voice. Sitting up straighter, she half turned to gaze at him. "I've never seduced a man before." A smile of unalloyed innocence curved her mouth. "Could you help me? If you don't mind, my lord," she demurely added.

A grin slowly creased his tanned cheek. "You play the ingenue well, Lady Graham," he said, sitting upright to better meet her frankly sensual gaze. His pale blue eyes had warmed, restoring a goodly measure of his charm. "I'd be a damned fool to mind," he said, his grin in sharp contrast to the curious affection in his eyes.

Exhaling theatrically, Elizabeth said, "Thank you, my lord," in a blatant parody of gratitude. "Without your assistance I despaired of properly arousing you."

He laughed, a warm-hearted sound of natural pleasure. "On that count you needn't have worried. I've been in rut since I left Edinburgh to see you."

"Could I be of some help?" she murmured, her voice husky, enticing.

He found himself attentively searching the ground for a suitable place to lie with her. "I warn you," he said very low, his mouth in a lazy grin, "I'm days past the need for seduction. All I can offer you is this country setting. Do you mind?"

She smiled up at him as she put her hand in his. "As long as you hold me, my lord, and as long as the grass stains don't show."

He paused for a moment with her small hand light on his palm. "You're very remarkable," he softly said.

"Too candid for you, my lord?" she playfully inquired.

His long fingers closed around her hand in an act of possession, pure and simple, as if he would keep this spirited, plain-speaking woman who startled him. "Your candor excites me," he said. "Be warned," he murmured, drawing her to her feet. "I've been wanting you for three days' past; I won't guarantee finesse." Releasing her hand, he held his up so she could see them tremble. "Look."

"I'm shaking *inside* so violently I may savage you first, my lord," Elizabeth softly breathed, swaying toward him, her fragrance sweet in his nostrils, her face lifted for a kiss. "I've been waiting four months since I left Goldiehouse."

A spiking surge of lust ripped through his senses, gut-deep, searing, her celibacy a singular, flamboyant ornament offered to him as if it were his duty, his obligation to bring her pleasure. In a flashing moment his hands closed on her shoulders. Pulling her sharply close, his palms slid down her back—then lower, swiftly cupping her bottom. His mouth dipped to hers and he forced her mouth open, plunging his tongue deep inside.

Like a woman too long denied, Elizabeth welcomed him, pulling his head down so she could reach his mouth more easily, straining upward on tiptoes so she could feel him hard against her, tearing at the buttons on his shirt so the heat of his skin touched hers.

"Hurry, Johnnie, please . . ." she whispered.

Moonlight, Madness, & Magic

by

Suzanne Foster, Charlotte Hughes, and Olivia Rupprecht

"A beguiling mix of passion and the occult. . . . an engaging read."
—*Publishers Weekly*
"Incredibly ingenious." —*Romantic Times*

This strikingly original anthology by three of Loveswept's bestselling authors is one of the most talked about books of the year! With more than 2.5 million copies of their titles in print, these beloved authors bring their talents to a boldly imaginative collection of romantic novellas that weaves a tale of witchcraft, passion, and unconditional love set in 1785, 1872, and 1992.

Here's a look at the heart-stopping prologue . . . .

OXFORD VILLAGE, MASSACHUSETTS — 1690 Rachael Deliverance Dobbs had been beautiful once. The flaming red hair that often strayed from her morning cap and curled in wispy tendrils about her face had turned more than one shop-keeper's head. Today, however, that red hair was tangled and filthy and fell against her back and shoulders like a tattered woolen shawl.

Prison had not served her well.

"The woman hath *witchcraft* in her," an onlooker spat out as Rachael was led to the front of the meeting house, where a constable, the governor's magistrate, and several of the town selectmen waited to decide her fate. Her ankles were shackled in irons, making her progress slow and painful.

Rachael staggered, struggling to catch her balance as the magistrate peered over his spectacles at her. Clearing his throat, the magistrate began to speak, giving each word a deep and thunderous import. "Rachael Deliverance Dobbs, thou hast been accused by this court of not fearing the Almighty God as do thy good and prudent neighbors, of preternatural acts against the citizenry of Oxford, and of the heinous crime of witchcraft, for which, by the law of the colony of Massachusetts, thou deservest to die. Has thou anything to say in thy defense?"

Rachael Dobbs could barely summon the strength to deny the charges. Her accusers had kept her jailed for months, often depriving her of sleep, food, and clean water to drink. In order to secure a confession, they'd whipped her with rawhide and tortured her with hideous instruments. Though she'd been grievously injured and several of her ribs broken, she'd given them nothing.

"Nay," she said faintly, "I know not of which ye speak, m'lord. For as God is my witness, I have been wrongly accused."

A rage quickened the air, and several of the spectators rose from their seats. "Blasphemy!" someone cried. "The witch would use *His* name in vain?"

"Order!" The magistrate brought his gavel down. "Let the accused answer the charges. Goody Dobbs, it is said thou makest the devil's brew of strange plants that grow in the forest."

"I know not this devil's brew you speak of," Rachael protested. "I use the herbs for healing, just as my mother before me."

"And thou extracts a fungus from rye grass to stop birthing pains?" he queried.

"I do not believe a woman should suffer so, m'lord."

"Even though the Good Book commands it?"

"The Good Book also commands us to use the sense God gave us," she reminded him tremulously.

"I'll not tolerate this sacrilege!" The village preacher slammed his fist down on the table, inciting the onlookers into a frenzy of shouting and name-calling.

As the magistrate called for order, Rachael turned to the crowd, searching for the darkly handsome face of her betrothed, Jonathan Nightingale. She'd not been allowed visitors in jail, but surely Jonathan would be here today to speak on her behalf. With his wealth and good name, he would quickly put an end to this hysteria. That hope had kept her alive, bringing her comfort even when she'd learned her children had been placed in the care of Jonathan's housekeeper, a young woman Rachael distrusted for her deceptive ways. But that mattered little now. When Jonathaan cleared her name of these crimes, she would be united with her babes once again. How she longed to see them!

"Speak thou for me, Jonathan Nightingale?" she cried, forgetting everything but her joy at seeing him. "Thou knowest me better than anyone. Thou knowest the secrets of my heart. Tell these people I am not what they accuse me. Tell them, so that my children may be returned to me." Her voice trembled with emotion, but as Jonathan glanced up and met her eyes, she knew a moment of doubt. She didn't see the welcoming warmth she expected. Was something amiss?

At the magistrate's instruction, the bailiff called Jonathan to come forward. "State thy name for the court," the bailiff said, once he'd been sworn in.

"Jonathan Peyton Nightingale."

"Thou knowest the accused, Goody Dobbs?" the magistrate asked.

Jonathan acknowledged Rachael with a slow nod of his head. "Mistress Dobbs and I were engaged to be married before she was incarcerated," Jonathan told the magistrate. "I've assumed the care of her children these last few months. She has no family of her own."

"Hast thou anything to say in her defense?"

"She was a decent mother, to be sure. Her children be well mannered."

"And have ye reason to believe the charges against her?"

When Jonathan hesitated, the magistrate pressed him. "Prithee, do not withhold information from the court, Mr. Nightingale," he cautioned, "lest thee find thyself in the same dire predicament as the accused. Conspiring to protect a witch is a lawful test of guilt."

Startled, Jonathan could only stare at the stern-faced tribunal before him. It had never occured to him that his association with Rachael could put him in a hangman's noose as well. He had been searching his soul since she'd been jailed, wondering how much he was morally bound to reveal at this trial. Now he saw little choice but to unburden himself.

"After she was taken, I found this among her things," he said, pulling an object from his coat pocket and unwrapping it. He avoided looking at Rachael, anticipating the stricken expression he would surely see in her eyes. "It's an image made of horsehair. A woman's image. There be a pin stuck through it."

The crowd gasped as Jonathan held up the effigy. A woman screamed, and even the magistrate drew back in horror.

Rachael sat in stunned disbelief. An icy fist closed around her heart. How could Jonathan have done such a thing? Did he not realize he'd signed her death warrant? Dear merciful God, if they found her guilty, she would never see her children again!

" 'Twas mere folly that I fashioned the image, m'lord," she told the magistrate. "I suspected my betrothed of dallying with his housekeeper. I fear my temper bested me."

"And was it folly when thou gavest Goodwife Brown's child the evil eye and caused her to languish with the fever?" the magistrate probed.

" 'Twas coincidence, m'lord," she said, imploring him to believe her. "The child was ill when I arrived at Goody Brown's house. I merely tried to help her." Rachael could see the magistrate's skepticism, and she whirled to Jonathan in desperation. "How canst thou doubt me, Jonathan?" she asked.

He hung his head. He was torn with regret, even shame. He loved Rachael, but God help him, he had no wish to die beside her. One had only to utter the word *witch* these days to end up on the gallows. Not that Rachael hadn't given all of them cause to suspect her. When he'd found the effigy, he'd told himself she must have been maddened by jealousy. But truly he didn't understand her anymore. She'd stopped going to Sunday services and more than once had induced him to lie abed with her on a Sabbath morn. "Methinks thou hast bewitched me as well, Rachael," he replied.

Another gasp from the crowd.

"Hanging is too good for her!" a woman shouted.

"Burn her!" another cried from the front row. "Before she bewitches us all."

Rachael bent her head in despair, all hope draining from her. Her own betrothed had forsaken her, and his condemnation meant certain death. There was no one who could save her now. And yet, in the depths of her desolation, a spark of rage kindled.

"So be it," she said, seized by a black hysteria. She was beyond caring now, beyond the crowd's censure or their grace. No one could take anything more from her than had already been taken. Jonathan's engagement gift to her, a golden locket, hung at her neck. She ripped it free and flung it at him.

"Thou shall have thy desire, Jonathan Nightingale," she cried. "And pay for it dearly. Since thou hast consigned me to the gallows and stolen my children from me, I shall put a blood curse on thee and thine."

The magistrate pounded his gavel against the table, ordering the spectators to silence. "Mistress Dobbs!" he warned, his voice harsh, "I fear thou hast just sealed thy fate."

But Rachael would not be deterred. Her heart was aflame with the fury of a woman betrayed. "Hear me good, Jonathan," she said, oblivious of the magistrate, of everyone but the man she'd once loved with all her being. "Thou hast damned my soul to hell, but I'll not burn there alone. I curse the Nightingale seed to a fate worse than the flames of Hades. Your progeny shall be as the living dead, denied the rest of the grave."

Her voice dropped to a terrifying hush as she began to intone the curse. "The third son of every third son shall walk the earth as a creature of the night, trapped in shadows, no two creatures alike. Stripped of humanity, he will howl in concert with demons, never to die, always to wander in agony, until a woman entraps his heart and soul as thee did mine—"

"My God, she is truly the devil's mistress!" the preacher gasped. A cry rose from the crowd, and several of them surged forward, trying to stop her. Guards rushed to block them.

"Listen to me, Jonathan!" Rachael cried over the din. "I've not finished with thee yet. If that woman should find a way to set the creature free, it will be at great and terrible cost. A sacrifice no mortal woman would ever be willing to make—"

She hesitated, her chin beginning to tremble as hot tears pooled in her eyes. Glistening, they slid down her cheeks, burning her tender flesh before they dropped to the wooden floor. But as they hit the planks, something astonishing happened. Even

Rachael in her grief was amazed. The teardrops hardened before everyone's eyes into precious gems. Flashing in the sunlight was a dazzling blue-white diamond, a blood-red ruby, and a brilliant green emerald.

The crowd was stunned to silence.

Rachael glanced up, aware of Jonathan's fear, of everyone's astonishment. Their gaping stares brought her a fleeting sense of triumph. Her curse had been heard.

"Rachael Dobbs, confess thy sins before this court and thy Creator!" the magistrate bellowed.

But it was too late for confessions. The doors to the courtroom burst open, and a pack of men streamed in with blazing pine torches. "Goody Brown's child is dead of the fits," they shouted. "The witch must burn!"

The guards couldn't hold back the vigilantes, and Rachael closed her eyes as the pack of men engulfed her. She said a silent good-bye to her children as she was gripped by bruising hands and lifted off the ground. She could feel herself being torn nearly apart as they dragged her from the meeting room, but she did not cry out. She felt no physical pain. She had just made a pact with the forces of darkness, and she could no longer feel anything except the white-hot inferno of the funeral pyre that would soon release her to her everlasting vigil.

She welcomed it, just as she welcomed the sweet justice that would one day be hers. She would not die in vain. Her curse had been heard.

"Fayrene Preston has an uncanny ability
to create intense atmosphere that
is truly superb."
—*Romantic Times*

Satin and Steele
by
Fayrene Preston

SATIN AND STEELE *is a classic favorite of fans of
Fayrene Preston. Originally published under the pseud-
onym Jaelyn Conlee, this novel was the talented Ms.
Preston's first ever published novel. We are thrilled to
offer you the opportunity to read this long-unavailable
book in its new Bantam edition.*

Skye Anderson knew the joy and wonder of love—as
well as the pain of its tragic loss. She'd carved a new
life for herself at Dallas' Hayes Corporation, finding
security in a cocoon of hard-working days and lonely
nights. Then her company is taken over by the leg-
endary corporate raider James Steele and once again
Skye must face the possibility of losing everything
she cares about. When Steele enlists her aid in
organizing the new company, she is determined to
prove herself worthy of the challenge. But as they
work together side by side, Skye can't deny that
she feels more than a professional interest in her

new boss—and that the feeling is mutual. Soon she would have to decide whether to let go of her desire for Steele once and for all—or risk everything for a second chance at love.

And don't miss these heart-stopping
romances from Bantam Books,
on sale in November:

ADAM'S FALL
a new hardcover edition of the Sandra
Brown classic!

NOTORIOUS
by Patricia Potter
The *Romantic Times* 1992
"Storyteller of the Year"

PRINCESS OF THIEVES
by Katherine O'Neal
"A brilliant new talent bound to make her
mark on the genre." —Iris Johansen

CAPTURE THE NIGHT
by Geralyn Dawson
"A fresh and delightful new author!
GOLD 5 stars"
—*Heartland Critiques*

and in hardcover from Doubleday

ON WINGS OF MAGIC
a classic romance by Kay Hooper

OFFICIAL RULES

To enter the sweepstakes below carefully follow all instructions found elsewhere in this offer.

The **Winners Classic** will award prizes with the following approximate maximum values: 1 Grand Prize: $26,500 (or $25,000 cash alternate); 1 First Prize: $3,000; 5 Second Prizes: $400 each; 35 Third Prizes: $100 each; 1,000 Fourth Prizes: $7.50 each. Total maximum retail value of Winners Classic Sweepstakes is $42,500. Some presentations of this sweepstakes may contain individual entry numbers corresponding to one or more of the aforementioned prize levels. To determine the Winners, individual entry numbers will first be compared with the winning numbers preselected by computer. For winning numbers not returned, prizes will be awarded in random drawings from among all eligible entries received. Prize choices may be offered at various levels. If a winner chooses an automobile prize, all license and registration fees, taxes, destination charges and, other expenses not offered herein are the responsibility of the winner. If a winner chooses a trip, travel must be complete within one year from the time the prize is awarded. Minors must be accompanied by an adult. Travel companion(s) must also sign release of liability. Trips are subject to space and departure availability. Certain black-out dates may apply.

The following applies to the sweepstakes named above:

No purchase necessary. You can also enter the sweepstakes by sending your name and address to: P.O. Box 508, Gibbstown, N.J. 08027. Mail each entry separately. Sweepstakes begins 6/1/93. Entries must be received by 12/30/94. Not responsible for lost, late, damaged, misdirected, illegible or postage due mail. Mechanically reproduced entries are not eligible. All entries become property of the sponsor and will not be returned.

Prize Selection/Validations: Selection of winners will be conducted no later than 5:00 PM on January 28, 1995, by an independent judging organization whose decisions are final. Random drawings will be held at 1211 Avenue of the Americas, New York, N.Y. 10036. Entrants need not be present to win. Odds of winning are determined by total number of entries received. Circulation of this sweepstakes is estimated not to exceed 200 million. All prizes are guaranteed to be awarded and delivered to winners. Winners will be notified by mail and may be required to complete an affidavit of eligibility and release of liability which must be returned within 14 days of date on notification or alternate winners will be selected in a random drawing. Any prize notification letter or any prize returned to a participating sponsor, Bantam Doubleday Dell Publishing Group, Inc., its participating divisions or subsidiaries, or the independent judging organization as undeliverable will be awarded to an alternate winner. Prizes are not transferable. No substitution for prizes except as offered or as may be necessary due to unavailability, in which case a prize of equal or greater value will be awarded. Prizes will be awarded approximately 90 days after the drawing. All taxes are the sole responsibility of the winners. Entry constitutes permission (except where prohibited by law) to use winners' names, hometowns, and likenesses for publicity purposes without further or other compensation. Prizes won by minors will be awarded in the name of parent or legal guardian.

Participation: Sweepstakes open to residents of the United States and Canada, except for the province of Quebec. Sweepstakes sponsored by Bantam Doubleday Dell Publishing Group, Inc., (BDD), 1540 Broadway, New York, NY 10036. Versions of this sweepstakes with different graphics and prize choices will be offered in conjunction with various solicitations or promotions by different subsidiaries and divisions of BDD. Where applicable, winners will have their choice of any prize offered at level won. Employees of BDD, its divisions, subsidiaries, advertising agencies, independent judging organization, and their immediate family members are not eligible.

Canadian residents, in order to win, must first correctly answer a time limited arithmetical skill testing question. Void in Puerto Rico, Quebec and wherever prohibited or restricted by law. Subject to all federal, state, local and provincial laws and regulations. For a list of major prize winners (available after 1/29/95): send a self-addressed, stamped envelope entirely separate from your entry to: Sweepstakes Winners, P.O. Box 517, Gibbstown, NJ 08027. Requests must be received by 12/30/94. DO NOT SEND ANY OTHER CORRESPONDENCE TO THIS P.O. BOX.